SON OF AN EARL

SON OF AN EARL
BROTHERHOOD OF THE BORDER

CECELIA MECCA

ALTIORA Press

To my "oops detection" team—Margaret, Lorrie, Joanna and Elaine. Thank you!

CHAPTER 1

B "You are unusually quiet, cousin." Conall leaned against the wall behind him and Hugh, goblet in hand, looking as pleased as one would expect of a man who'd just married the woman he loved.

Hugh nurtured his own goblet, enjoying the hard-won festivities as much as any. But thoughts of the woman he'd spied earlier continued to plague him.

"There is but one reason you neither smile nor take Isolda's maid to your chamber. Tell me," Conall pressed.

Hugh did not wish to burden his cousin on his wedding day, so he distracted him instead. "As I've said, my affair with the maid has run its course."

"There are other women here, many of whom look your way even now. The Hugh I know does not scowl in the corner with such possibilities before him. He runs with reivers, angers his parents, and laughs even when everyone around him frowns."

"I will not dispute your words, cousin. As for the

1

women. . . they are noble. Virgins. None of whom I would dare touch in your wife's hall." He corrected himself. "Your hall."

Despite his cousin's Scots origins, he was now wed to an Englishwoman and would rule Bramton alongside her.

"The one smiling at you from beside the musicians. She is a widow."

And a pretty one at that. He sighed, uninterested.

"Since you will not cease your matchmaking, and I would prefer a new topic, it is the hooded woman my father spotted earlier whom I think of now."

Conall's brows raised. "Indeed?"

"For no other reason than she hides her face. When I thought to approach her, the woman disappeared. Do you not think it odd?"

"That she was hooded or that she disappeared?"

"Both. My father made some inquiries and discovered that her name is Lady Criseyde di Vilardino, from Venice apparently. She is a guest of Bramton's priest."

"A nun, perhaps?"

"Nay," he replied, taking a sip of wine. At Conall's concerned expression, he sought to reassure him. Isolda would not be pleased that he distracted his cousin on his wedding day. "Do not give the matter another thought. I am being as fanciful as a squire on the eve before he earns his spurs."

Conall smiled. "I remember the day clearly when you earned yours."

Their families, once bitter enemies, were now as intertwined as any along the border. When Hugh's uncle married into Clan Kerr more than thirty years ago, he had sparked the beginnings of an allegiance that now formed a corridor of safe passage in the region from England to Scotland. With this marriage, their Brotherhood had only become more powerful.

"No doubt you also remember what happened later that eve?"

Conall pretended to think back to that day when they had been but young men. "Nay, I do not recall." As his cousin had lost his virginity to a young English widow, Hugh doubted his memory lapsed so thoroughly. But since this was Conall's wedding feast, he would not force the memory from him. "How long will you stay?"

"I plan to return to Kenshire on the morrow with my parents to prepare for the Northumbria Council."

"You've a king to pacify thanks to me," Conall said apologetically.

Hugh slapped his cousin on his shoulder as he caught Isolda's eye. She looked for her new husband, and he would relinquish Conall to her.

"No more talk of politics tonight. I know that look well." He indicated Lady Isolda. "Your wife awaits."

"I've a surprise for her," Conall admitted. "We've been long enough in the hall," he said, finishing the remainder of his wine and handing the goblet to Hugh.

"Am I a serving maid now?" he asked as Conall walked away. His cousin lifted his arm in parting, not bothering to answer. The moment he did so, Hugh turned away, dropping his smile, and once again looked through the hall.

He should forget the woman, do as Conall advised, and ask the blonde widow for a dance. But there had been something about her that Hugh could not dismiss.

A hooded woman, alone, unescorted. On its own, perhaps not enough to concern him. But he could not dismiss the prickle that rose up his back as he watched Lady Criseyde di Vilardino in the shadows.

His decision made, Hugh placed both goblets on a nearby trestle table, and began to move toward her.

CHAPTER 2

"You are back so soon, my lady?"

Elizabeth opened the door for her, though it was not necessary. Criseyde had told her maid many times that she could manage her personal matters, including such things as opening a door, but the woman insisted.

Only two years younger than she, the maid, also having lost her husband to the sickness that tore through France the year before, had little else in common with Criseyde. Even so, they had gotten on well enough these past ten years that when she accepted this mission to come to England, Elizabeth was the only person she asked to accompany her.

Despite King Philip's objections.

"Aye." Criseyde entered the chamber that she'd occupied since coming to Bramton. Elizabeth slept in an adjoining chamber in the monastery, where they'd been welcomed a sennight earlier. "There was a man," she began, stopping.

What could she say?

5

A man that had stirred something in her that Criseyde had not known was possible?

After her father had betrothed her to Etienne du Castel, she'd ceased looking at men the way she had before. Then, afterward, she did not wish to dishonor her late husband, even if their union had been one of advantage and not love. Her year of mourning had passed long ago, as had her desire to be with another man again.

"A man?" Elizabeth prompted.

Criseyde attempted to describe him. "Aye. The second son of Lord Waryn, Earl of Kenshire. He looked at me as if. . ."

Elizabeth watched her. Criseyde was rarely unable to find words to express her thoughts. "As if he knew something," she finished.

Which was true enough.

Though she'd been timid when they met, when the king himself offered Elizabeth's service after Criseyde and her father arrived at court, her maid had taken on many of Criseyde's mannerisms, including crossing her arms the way she did now.

"We've not gone a day on this journey without you believing someone knows more than they should. But never have you looked this way."

Criseyde thought of his face. His jaw, that looked as if it were carved from marble. His eyes, so suspicious. She could see that even beneath her hood. And the man's stance, as if he were the Earl of Bramton and not his cousin.

Aye, he was suspicious for certain. Perhaps she should not have gone to the wedding feast hooded, as too few Englishwomen seemed to prefer the fashion that had been more commonplace in France lately. But neither did she wish to invite any of the guests to speak with her. Criseyde was there to observe and nothing more.

"He was. . ." She hesitated, and then offered, "Different." Criseyde removed her cloak, waving Elizabeth off, and began to take off her boots as well.

"Different," her maid pressed. "How?"

Criseyde had been raised by a physician, the councillor of the Repubblica di Venezia, and a man daring enough to leave his home country to become the French king's personal astrologer. Her cheeks did not redden. She did not retreat from conversations.

Until now.

"I am tired," she lied. "'Tis late, and tomorrow I will see the blacksmith. 'Tis said he has grown close to the new lord and perhaps I can gain information from him."

"Tired. Hmm." Elizabeth would not question her, but she clearly wanted to. It seemed she would receive her wish, as her maid appeared to be preparing to leave. "You learned nothing this eve, then?"

"Nay," she replied. "I was able to listen to a conversation between two of the new lord's men that I thought might offer more than it did. Indeed, the men seem interested in little besides getting under the skirts of women."

Elizabeth's eyes narrowed. "Speaking of getting under women's skirts—"

"We will talk of no such thing." Criseyde stopped Elizabeth short. Not because the discussion made her feel shameful. But because her maid had guessed the true reason the earl's son had so fettered Criseyde this eve.

A subject neither woman had time to dwell on, as the future of Scotland could very well be in their hands. An attraction to Sir Hugh of Kenshire was of no consequence, but her purpose here was.

CHAPTER 3

He hadn't dared speak to the priest.

By all accounts, from what Hugh had learned, the man had not just welcomed Lady Criseyde but protected her. Hugh spoke to the stablemaster, who he had come to know during his stay at Bramton. The man knew as much as any other here, so he'd not been surprised to gain more information from him last eve.

He recalled their discussion as Hugh waited for the lady to emerge from her chamber. "She arrived a sennight ago," the stablemaster had said. "It is common, as you know, for the monastery to receive guests, but Lady Criseyde seems particularly close to Father Godwin."

Though Hugh's father had been the first person to notice her, when Hugh reported his findings he'd not seemed particularly concerned. Perhaps she was no threat to Conall and Isolda, but still Hugh could not forget how quickly she'd disappeared when they'd paid her notice. Never again would he dismiss a potential threat. Doing so had nearly cost Hugh his life.

The door finally creaked open. And this time, she wore no hood.

Bloody hell, the woman was beautiful.

Pushing away from the stone wall, he made himself known to her. Criseyde's brown eyes widened as she noticed him for the first time. Her breath caught, and Hugh understood. It was as if the air around them crackled, like a flame that had finally found a dry log to latch onto.

"Sir Hugh," she said, her voice matching everything about the woman. Lady Criseyde was unlike most English maids. Her skin had never been shielded from the sun, it seemed, though it somehow remained smooth. At least, Hugh imagined it would be so. The urge to touch her cheek was as unbidden as it was improper. As was his inability to look away from her unusually full lips.

If she'd been unhooded and not acting so suspiciously last eve, every man in that hall would have asked the lady for a dance, himself included. There had been no mention of a husband, but that did not mean she was unwed.

"Lady Criseyde." He used her name as deliberately as she had used his. "It seems we know each other without having met."

If she was surprised Hugh knew her identity, she did not show it.

"How did you get into this corridor? I was assured it was closed to all but myself and my maid?"

"The question you should be asking, my lady, is why am I here?"

Her eyes narrowed. "You looked at me last eve," she said. A fair strategy, telling Hugh what he already knew.

"Indeed I did. Though you hide yourself well."

"Not well enough if you stand before me asking questions," she shot back.

She was annoyed with him, rightly so. But what surprised him most was that Criseyde did not hide it. "Why?"

"I should not think I must explain myself to you. A stranger."

"Though you know who I am, so not completely a stranger to you."

Unlike his brothers, Hugh had not trained at Kenshire alone. His was a more. . . unconventional training. One he was suddenly thankful for, as trading barbs was a skill he'd honed well with his father's friends. And it seemed a skill he'd need in dealing with her.

"I know your name," she replied, "hardly the man behind it."

Would you like to?

He did not say it aloud. Hugh would not flirt with a woman who may be married, nor did he wish to flirt with Lady Criseyde. It was information he wanted from her, nothing more.

"Ask me any question you like."

"Why are you here?"

"Except that one."

"How did you get in here unnoticed?"

"'Tis easy to hide among the shadows when no one is looking for you."

"I could scream," she threatened.

"Yet you will not."

She cocked her head to the side. "You think not?"

"I know it well. You are aware my cousin is now Earl of Bramton. If you screamed, all may come running, but in the end we would be brought before him and Isolda. Surely you do not wish to cause such grief to a newly wedded couple?"

Her eyes—intelligent and guarded—remained steadfastly intent on him. "My maid is breaking her fast even now. She will be waiting for me."

Indeed, the maid would eventually come looking for her lady. "Why do you attend my cousin's wedding feast alone, unchaperoned, and hooded as if to avoid notice?"

"I attended the wedding because Father Godwin asked if I would like to do so as his guest. I was not unchaperoned, and the hood would not have attracted notice were we at court."

By her accent, it was clear the court she referred to was in France.

"Born in Venice, residing in France long enough to gain the accent you now speak with, and you are here, along the border, the guest of Bramton's priest."

"Your observations sound as if they are accusations."

Hugh shrugged, eyes remaining on her face. He could hear his mother's voice telling him and his brothers they would receive a smack on the back of their heads each and every time they dared stare at a woman's bosom, and not her face, when she was speaking.

He'd received more smacks than either Haydn or Holt. Not because Holt deserved them any less than he, but because his younger brother was more adept at hiding his attentions.

"Why did you leave when you noticed me watching you?"

Again, she did not flinch. "You think the two are related?"

"I know they are."

Her chin rose. "You are too bold, Sir Hugh. If you will pardon me, I would break my fast." She began to walk away.

Hugh did not even consider stopping her. Instead, he

simply locked his step to her own. But that did give her pause.

"You would come with me?"

"Aye, my lady."

"Why?'

Hugh offered a bit of truth. "Because I do not trust you. There is something amiss about your presence here at Bramton, and I mean to discover what it is."

He watched her closely. And was impressed by her calm. The woman betrayed nothing.

"Do as you will," she said. "But you will learn I am merely traveling through Bramton."

"Traveling to where?"

This time, she did bristle a bit. "That is not of your concern, my lord."

"I disagree," Hugh responded as Lady Criseyde stopped walking to glower at him. "You knew my name, which means you know my family, as well as my cousin Conall's. A threat to any Waryn, or Kerr, is a threat to every member of our Brotherhood. I would no sooner dismiss such a threat than I would were my own life in danger. So aye, it is as much my concern as it would be my cousin's were it not the day after his wedding, and I were to tell him of you."

While he spoke, she'd regained her composure. Lifting her skirts once again, Lady Criseyde said evenly, "I am no threat. To you, to your cousin, or to Bramton. Good day, my lord."

With that, she walked away from him. This time, he did not follow.

Hugh had someone to speak to instead.

CHAPTER 4

"You are certain this is necessary, my lady?"

Criseyde was not certain at all. In fact, when they arrived at Bramton and she'd learned there was a new earl, a member of Clan Kerr, no less, she thought perhaps their journey might be coming to an end. Instead, it seemed as if Father Godwin's initial advice when they arrived would now be their next course of action. They would travel north, across the border, into Sutwork.

"I am certain of little," she said to Elizabeth, mounting. "But we were advised to use caution and will observe that advice now."

The men with whom they traveled had already mounted. When they turned back to her, Criseyde nodded and the four of them set off. Having bid adieu to the priest who'd been sympathetic to their cause, they rode from the monastery north, away from Bramton Castle.

Away from Sir Hugh and his questions.

Or so Lady Criseyde had thought. No sooner had they passed through the gates than a rider approached from behind. Criseyde turned only because of the speed of the horse, whom all four of them could hear clearly.

Muttering a curse under her breath, one she'd learned from the king of France himself, Criseyde called to her companions to stop.

"You failed to mention you were leaving so soon," the same man she'd been thinking about since that morn called out. Since the moment Criseyde had discovered him outside her chamber, she'd known two things quite clearly.

First, Sir Hugh suspected her.

Second, he was the most compelling man she had ever met.

For a woman who had spent time at court in three countries, who had met what some had considered the most interesting people in the world, the very thought was absurd. But also true. He looked less like the son of an earl than one of the many men they'd met on the road, ones wishing to test her companion's skills and relieve Elizabeth of their purses, or more.

Dark and dangerous were the two words that had come to mind in the hall at the wedding feast, and today Criseyde realized, unfortunately, how right she had been to think them.

"We meet again, my lady," he said, catching up to them. Criseyde pulled the folds of her mantle tight. It would be a long, cold day ahead, and she did not wish to make it more so by speaking to him. If not for Sir Hugh they would be warm inside the monastery, Criseyde ensuring there were no further leads to follow here at Bramton.

"It seems," she said, slowing her mount as the others did the same, "we do not simply meet here. But instead, you sought me out, my lord?"

He feigned confusion. His mantle dark, like the rest of

him, Sir Hugh wore no gloves, as if daring the weather to tangle with him. "You are a suspicious sort to believe so."

"We should continue to move, my lady."

At the sound of Ranald's voice, Sir Hugh gave her man his full attention. His expression changed very quickly from mild amusement to suspicion.

"You are far from the shores of France," Hugh accused.

Ranald, like Bernard and Elizabeth, knew well the details of their mission. And of the stakes for the wrong person to learn of it. Namely, likely death to all four of them and two, if not three, countries at war.

"Indeed," he said, revealing nothing. "Shall we continue, Lady Criseyde?" Ranald asked her as if Sir Hugh did not exist.

"I bid you a good day," she began, but Sir Hugh would not be so easily dismissed.

"I would know your business here at Bramton," he demanded of Ranald.

"You are the new earl's cousin," Ranald said smoothly. "For that reason, I will not take offense at the rudeness of your question. My lady?"

He had been chosen for this mission for that precise reason. The man was as smooth and understated, yet effective, as any. In some ways, he reminded Criseyde of her late husband. Neither were men who looked, like Sir Hugh, as if they would welcome a fight. Unlike Etienne, however, Ranald was better prepared to actually engage a man like Sir Hugh in swordplay. Her husband had been more scholar than swordsman, like her father. The only quality they shared.

Pushing aside the thought, not willing to allow fond memories of the man that had raised her to interfere with her judgment now, Criseyde attempted to put an end to the discussion.

"We are leaving Bramton," she said firmly. "Our destination should be of little concern to you."

"Your destination, perhaps not. Your purpose here is another story indeed." Hugh was no longer speaking in innuendos.

Neither would she. "I answer to many men," she said, weary of the fact. "But you are not one of them."

This time, as she attempted to ignore him and ride ahead, Sir Hugh positioned himself so that she was unable to do so. Immediately the others dismounted and were at her side, swords drawn.

That did little to pacify him. The man she'd met outside her chamber this morn, the one who had even smiled before, among guests at his cousin's wedding, was nowhere to be found. Sir Hugh's expression had transformed so quickly that Criseyde could not be certain she looked at the same man.

"We've done nothing to warrant your suspicions," she said, her voice steady.

"Says a woman surrounded by two French knights who do not bear the markings of their station."

She did not ask how he'd guessed as much. Their stances now, and the quality of their swords, was enough to recommend anyone who cared to notice either.

"Two women traveling alone necessitate such protection."

"Lower your weapons," he said to her companions. "You will accompany me to the keep and explain your presence here at Bramton."

"We will do no such thing," she said. "We were guests of Father Godwin."

"Were. You are no longer his ward but are now on Bramton land."

Indeed, they were. "You have been waiting to ambush me."

"I have been watching you, aye," he admitted. "With good reason, it seems."

She should have been more forthright this morn, but his questioning had irked her—the very thing King Philip had warned her against when she'd asked to undertake this mission. And now that emotion would work against them.

Sighing, she bid the men to lower their weapons. "I am to reunite with my husband at Edinburgh, where his business has been delayed," she said, "and these men have journeyed with me for protection. We were waylaid at Brampton by a storm, have worn out our welcome, and now seek to be on our way."

She did not miss the look that passed across his features at the mention of her husband.

"You could not have said as much this morn?"

"I did not wish to."

"Perhaps you should have done so. Now you can explain it to the Lord and Lady of Bramton."

What a most stubborn, irritating man.

"Why must we do so?"

He was quick to answer. "Because I do not believe you."

"And you would detain us because of your fickle notions?"

His eyes flashed. "Your insults mean little to me, my lady. The truth, on the other hand, means a great deal. And you offer little of it."

"You would detain us from leaving?" Ranald asked, incredulous.

17

"In the name of the Earl of Bramton," Sir Hugh said, his hand on the hilt of the sword at his waist still. "I would."

They had no other choice now. Perhaps she should have waited, but Criseyde had been certain Sir Hugh was no longer at the monastery. How could she have known he'd been lurking all day? And now she would have to offer more of the story they'd devised, one she'd only been forced to tell twice before.

"We will be on our way soon enough," she told her companions. "Do as he bids."

But the look he gave her now said just the opposite. Criseyde was concerned, aye, but not overly so. It was an inconvenience, but they would be headed north soon enough.

CHAPTER 5

H is cousin was going to kill him.

"You did what?" Conall paced the solar chamber after listening to Hugh's tale. He'd considered speaking to Gregory, the steward who handled much of Bramton's affairs, especially in the aftermath of Conall and Isolda's wedding, but the man had been inexplicably absent from the hall and could not be found anywhere.

"Perhaps our Italian, French lady has had him kidnapped," Conall had said sarcastically when Hugh explained the situation. Hugh had been clear all those years ago when the ransom had been paid and he had been freed from his tormentors. . . he would not let the incident shape him. Kidnapping was commonplace along the border. Indeed, Conall's wife Isolda had been kidnapped by her own marshal, who cared not for Isolda and her father's politics.

Nay, he would have just the opposite. Jesting about his own ordeal had made it easier for Hugh to relive the memories.

"Would you have me ignore my instincts?"

Conall glowered at him. Hugh understood. He'd not have wished to be pulled from his wife's bed either for such an incident. Except, the woman sharing his bed would not be a wife. Instead, she would be a widow, yearning for a man's touch once again. A vision of the woman they now discussed came to him, as it had many times since he had first spoken to Lady Criseyde outside her chamber in the monastery.

The *married* Lady Criseyde.

He'd not been expecting that announcement. As she traveled alone, with no mention of a husband during his inquiries, he'd assumed she was either unmarried or a widow. A pity, she was neither.

"Nay," Conall said begrudgingly. "I would not. Though I cannot see the threat they pose if your lady was leaving Bramton."

"My lady," he said sardonically, "is a liar. I cannot discern truth from lie as she speaks. The fact remains that she was sulking among your guests, left when my father and I paid her notice, and then attempted to flee after I questioned her this morn."

"Your father," Conall said, "is none too pleased, I am told, for having been delayed."

Hugh winced. He'd delayed his parents from returning to Kenshire that morn and then returned from the monastery announcing he would remain at Bramton even longer, not accompanying them to Kenshire as planned. When he'd explained his reasoning, even his father, who had first spied the lady in the hall, thought Hugh was being overly cautious. As Conall did now.

"Is there perhaps another reason you've detained the woman?"

Hugh feigned surprise. "You wound me, cousin."

"Hugh?"

When he saw Lady Criseyde, his cousin would not be pleased. "My reputation aside—"

"As if I could separate the man from his misdeeds."

Hugh ignored that. "She is married, or so she claims."

Conall immediately changed his stance. Not one member of either of their families would dishonor a woman, or her husband, in that way. "You do not believe her?"

"I believe only that something is amiss."

Conall sighed, shook his head, and then nodded toward the door. "Then let us attend to the matter before Isolda is alerted of any trouble. She is riding with her mother, and I would leave her to it."

They were partway to the hall when Hugh stopped his cousin. Though only through marriage, each of the Waryn men and women considered themselves cousin—or aunt or uncle—without distinction. A long way from the bitter feud that had separated the Waryns and Clan Scott so many years ago.

"I've a memory," he said, "of walking behind my father and yours in just this manner. We were at Kenshire. Your father had come for a council meeting when my own found it necessary to address a messenger from the king. They seemed so large to me, these powerful men striding through the corridor. I remember being afraid for the messenger. They appeared so angry at the time."

"Likely because they were." Conall laughed. "My father bears less love for Edward than even yours does."

As his wards, Hugh's parents had been forced to dance to the English king's tune when necessary, even though they, and all of the borderland lords, cared little for the politics of the South. But Conall's father, second-in-command to his clan, paid no such homage, of course. Alex Kerr, of all the brothers, was as aligned with the Scots' bid for independence from Edward's interference as any.

"Aye," he agreed. "But when did we become… them?"

Conall finally understood his meaning. "We are no longer merely the sons of great men."

He could never be as great as his father, but it was not a slight against himself. None of them could. And yet, here they stood. "I'll not regret a decision once made," he said, aware he was defending himself even when it was unnecessary.

"Then let's get to it," Conall said as they continued to the hall.

With guards at the entrance, a very angry party of four stood in its center. The tables had been cleared after the midday meal, and Bramton's hall appeared much larger for it.

"Apologies for the delay," Conall said, addressing Lady Criseyde. "My cousin had cause for concerns which we would address before you were on your way."

The lady's eyes flashed angrier than he'd seen them yet.

God, the woman was beautiful. Though Hugh could not decide if her husband was lucky or unlucky to be married to such a striking, passionate woman.

"I demand we be allowed to leave this hall immediately."

Unlucky, for certain.

"As you will," Conall said. "But first, if it pleases you, explain your presence here at Bramton. I understand you were a guest of our monastery?"

Our monastery. It was odd, Hugh never imagined Conall anywhere other than Scotland, but now he counted himself an English earl. What plans were in his own future that Hugh was not aware of? Or did man make his own fate? It was something he often considered.

"As a guest of Father Godwin's, I would expect to be above reproach even if he"—she shot Hugh a most unkind glance—"is affronted by my presence."

"I am not affronted by your presence," Hugh said. "The opposite is true, in fact, as I find your presence intriguing. That you attempted to flee after being questioned is the reason for our suspicion."

"Your suspicion," she corrected.

"What say you?" Conall asked the unusually quiet men at her side. Ranald, he believed, was her companion's name.

"We offer the Lady Criseyde protection."

She ranked above them. Was in command. If that had not been clear before, it was so now.

The lady in question raised her chin. "I am Lady Criseyde di Vilardino. My father was Tommaso di Benvenuto da Pizzano, a physician and councillor in the Republic of Venice. He accepted an appointment to the French court of King Philip as his astrologer, at which time we lived in Paris. My husband is the notary and royal secretary Etienne du Castel and currently in Edinburgh, where we travel to meet him."

A pretty speech, and perhaps partially true, but there were falsehoods in her statements as well. The maid seemed surprised. No less than he was to learn of the lady's most esteemed upbringing. But there were still many questions, certainly, one of which his cousin seemed prepared to ask.

"You travel to meet your husband in winter? The cause must indeed be urgent?"

Hugh thought much the same.

"Indeed," she answered. "I've word he is ill."

He and Conall exchanged a glance. His cousin seemed content with her explanation, but he was not.

"You fled from the wedding feast when I watched you. You fled today from the monastery when I questioned you. Why?"

"Perhaps I do not care for your presence, Sir Hugh."

Conall actually smiled.

"A lie if there ever was one," he countered.

"Can you not discern the difference between truth and lie? If you could, you would know easily I've less desire to remain in the same hall as you as I do to travel through the Carnwood Mountains now after such a delay."

"Then perhaps you should not have fled so quickly."

"Or perhaps you should not have stopped us for no other reason than your unnatural curiosity."

"Perhaps," he started, but Conall stopped him.

"My lady," he said, "a storm is brewing. It grows late for such a journey. Remain here as my guests for the evening and part in the morn."

Hugh would never question his cousin's judgment in his own hall, but Hugh thought Conall was making a mistake.

For the first time since they met, Lady Criseyde smiled at Hugh. It was a victorious smile, one filled with contempt.

He did not smile back.

After whispering to her companions, the lady agreed and was escorted from the hall with a parting glance at him. Hugh ignored her.

"Come," Conall said. "We must speak in private."

He peered through the hall and into the corridor one last time.

Lady Criseyde had chosen that moment to look back at him as well. It was the very same look his sister Haddie had given him many times, just before she stuck out her tongue at him when they were younger.

The difference between Haddie and Criseyde? His sister knew that Hugh did not give up so easily, but this Italian-born and French-bred woman did not.

Yet.

CHAPTER 6

T
his was likely madness.

His father would be waiting for him at Kenshire. In less than a sennight, all of the border lords in Northumbria would meet there to discuss the problem of their king. While others did not have as much of a target on them as their family did for being so closely aligned to Clan Kerr, among other infractions, all agreed King Edward had become more fanatical of late when it came to subduing the Scots.

William Wallace had been defeated and was in hiding. There had been no major battles all winter. And yet the king continued to order to attack across the border, to "harangue the insolent Scots until north of the border bled with their insolence."

Few had the desire to do so. The king failed, as he'd done for years like his father before him, to understand the borderers. None wished to give their lives for a cause that only one man was passionate to carry.

Hugh should be there for that meeting, and yet, here he

was instead hiding in the shadows, following a party of four north. Decidedly not toward Edinburgh. At first it seemed the lady had at least told that truth, but by mid-afternoon, he'd not been surprised when they turned west. Hugh had nearly confronted her then but decided against it. He'd not wished to travel farther away from the eastern shores where Kenshire Castle awaited. But knowing he'd been right, that Lady Criseyde had not been truthful about her purpose at Bramton, Hugh was determined to see his suspicions through.

The storm that had threatened yesterday never came to pass, and although it was cold, the terrain had remained mostly flat, making for an easy ride thus far.

But all that was about to change.

From their direction, Hugh assumed Lady Criseyde and her companions headed to Sutwork, which they would reach easily by nightfall. Unfortunately, however, they were no longer the only travelers on this old Roman road.

He'd spotted them earlier on the ridge in front of them, and it seemed the reckoning would come sooner than expected. The riders, six or seven from what he could discern, were nearly upon Lady Criseyde's party.

Smiling, now recognizing them as he could see the reivers clearly, Hugh slowed his mount to watch the scene unfold. They exchanged words, though he could hear none of what was said from here. At least the lady was wise enough to travel lightly, but their packhorse would be cause enough for them to be stopped. As he suspected, the men appeared to inspect Lady Criseyde's belongings.

Which was when one of the lady's knights forced Hugh to intervene. He'd been hoping the pair of French fools would keep their swords sheathed.

Bollocks, but this woman proved difficult.

"Nay," she screamed, "there is naught of value there." Then, to her man, "Ranald, put down your weapon."

Smart woman.

"Listen to Lady Criseyde," Hugh bellowed as he emerged, not having yet been spotted.

He enjoyed watching her face as the lady, her companions, and the Roberts clan all gaped at him.

"As wily as they come," Ulric said, now ignoring the others. He dismounted, as Hugh did, and embraced him as if Hugh were a long-lost brother. Which, in many ways, he was.

"You would be dead," Hugh said, his hand still on the older man's shoulder, "had I wished it. Best you be more careful—"

"What in the name of the lord are you doing here? And embracing the man who attempted to rob us?"

Hugh ignored her.

"You know them?" Ulric asked.

"Aye. Have been following them from Bramton." At the reiver's confused look, he shook his head. "A tale for another time."

"Put down your sword," Hugh repeated the lady's words to her man. "Now," he bellowed more forcefully as the Frenchman did not do so immediately.

He'd managed to surprise the man enough for him to follow his orders. Even Lady Criseyde said nothing, perhaps realizing she'd made a mistake in thinking these men simply robbers.

They were that, and more. If Ulric and his men perceived a threat, they'd not hesitate to kill Lady Criseyde's man. Some may call them murderers, aye, but here, along the border, a decision to keep a man alive could be the cause of your own demise.

"We cannae have the trunk," one of Ulric's companions said. A Scotsman, one Hugh did not recognize, lowered his eyes as Ulric stared at him.

"Scots," Ulric muttered.

"Why does he run with you?" Hugh asked, approaching the other reivers.

"Married William's daughter, much to his ire."

Hugh laughed. It served the man right. William was intolerant as any of their northern neighbors. He and Hugh had gotten into more than one argument over the matter.

He moved from man to man, all mounted, greeting each, asking for their families and gaining news from across the border, where they'd apparently been raiding these past days.

Eventually Lady Criseyde had enough of Hugh's reunion with his father's old friends, now his own. . . men he himself had ridden with many times.

"Many thanks for the rescue," she said to Hugh, "but we would be on our way."

Both he and Ulric turned to stare at her.

"She is a beauty," Ulric whispered, though not so quietly, to him.

"Indeed," Hugh said. "Though married."

"Och, a shame. 'Tis time you marry now too since Haydn has taken a wife."

"I'd not make the same mistake as my brother, and certainly not with a woman who is incapable of telling one word of truth."

She could not argue with him now. It was clear their destination was not Edinburgh. Was she indeed married?

Most importantly, what had Lady Criseyde been doing at Bramton at Isolda and Conall's wedding feast?

"Are we once again your captives, or are we free to leave?"

Ulric winced. He knew better than any that Hugh would never take a man, or woman, captive except in the most necessary of circumstances. The woman had remained in Bramton's keep, a guest. She and her companions had dined as Conall further inquired into the lady's stay and spoke to the priest. Then, determining Hugh had been overly suspicious, he'd allowed her and her companions to leave that morn.

Hardly captives, though it appeared now such might have been warranted.

"She has questions to answer," he told Ulric, "but you can leave her and her party in my care."

"As you would," the reiver said, mounting once again. "Give your father our regards when you see him next."

"The same to your family," Hugh said, waving as the group rode south away from them. Good men, most of them, just trying to survive.

"They were border reivers," Lady Criseyde said as the last of them rode away. "I've heard tales of them before."

"Given you ride along the border with naught but two escorts"—he nodded to the two useless Frenchman—"I am glad to hear you are at least not so ignorant that you did not know you were in danger today."

Her eyes narrowed. "I've not met an Englishman yet less gentlemanly than you."

"Says the woman whose property was just rescued from said man. I believe you meant to offer thanks but spouted vitriol instead."

"Go to hell, Sir Hugh."

The woman certainly did not shy from epithets. "Only if you will show me the way?"

This time, she did not ask but spurred her mount forward, leaving him laughing despite his increasingly dour mood. Hugh followed, supposing it was time for answers.

Of the more truthful kind.

CHAPTER 7

You should not have offered yourself for this mission.

It was not the first time she'd had the thought, but as Criseyde rode away from Sir Hugh, it was truly the first time she believed it. With all to gain and naught to lose, she'd foolishly insisted to the king that she was the woman he sought to bring his message to the outlaw William Wallace.

The king of France had decided to support the Scots cause.

After yet another row with the king of England, Philip had been infuriated enough to reconsider Wallace's earlier request. By now, however, Wallace would be back in Scotland, so a message would need to be sent to him.

Her orders from the king were clear.

None but the man himself could receive the message.

Leaving Paris with naught but two guards, her maid, and a list of names she'd been forced to put to memory—people who were known sympathizers to the Scots cause—she had left the French court behind on what would prove to be her greatest adventure of all.

It had gone smoothly, despite the weather. Philip had been clear. Aye, a woman and daughter of a court astrologist would gain little notice as a royal messenger. And she was as trusted by the king as any man or woman at court. Since her funds had grown low after her father and then husband's death, Criseyde had not hesitated to offer her services.

Perhaps she should have done so.

Though not on her list of men she could trust to inquire about Wallace's whereabouts, the more she'd learned about Clan Kerr, the more Criseyde had begun to believe Conall, now the earl of Bramton, may have been a man she could have spoken openly to. Before she could determine as much for herself, they'd been forced to flee.

Courtesy of the man who'd just caught up to her.

"You will tell me the truth," he said, now riding alongside her.

"Or?" she replied, biding time she no longer had. Criseyde looked back to find her men, but they were nowhere to be found.

"I told them if I spotted either one of them, I would ride back and send my friends back. So there will be no rescue, Lady Criseyde."

"I need no rescue," she said with false bravado. Thankfully, the weather continued to hold, and Ranald, who was raised in these borderlands—the reason he'd been chosen for this mission—told her they'd reach Sutwork Manor well before the sun set. But Criseyde saw no sign of it, or of a way to avoid Sir Hugh's questions.

"Do you not? It appeared otherwise to me earlier. Or did you have the situation in hand, do you believe?"

She did not, of course. But neither would Criseyde admit as much. One thing she'd learned at an early age. . .

as a woman, any sign of hesitation was seen as weakness. She had written on the subject, much to her father's dismay. Most did not dare to speak the truth, and the truth was that women were regarded as little more than cattle, and she meant to change that.

But Criseyde was a long way from sharing her thoughts, and words, among the French nobles. Instead, she'd somehow managed to traverse first by sea and now by land much farther from home than she'd ever expected.

Surprisingly, when she did not respond, her companion did not do so either. She peeked from the corner of her eye at him.

Sir Hugh made quite a sight, indeed. His mantle was black, like the mount he rode, and there was an axe hanging from near his saddlebag, the likes of which she'd never seen before. When he looked at her, Criseyde averted his gaze and stared straight ahead at the frozen road in front of them.

Heart racing, she attempted to contrive a new story, one that would account for them not having headed toward Edinburgh, but her mind would not allow it. Instead, she could think only of him. Of this infuriating man beside her.

Criseyde could not tell him the truth.

While he was aligned by marriage to Clan Kerr, and her inquires suggested the Waryn family sympathized with the Scots cause, her instructions from the king had been clear.

"Speak Wallace's name to no one unless you are as certain about their intentions as your desire to see this mission completed."

She was less certain about Sir Hugh than she had been of Conall Kerr. Yet she could think of no lie that would convince this man to stop following her.

"My husband is dead," she began. Some truth was necessary. "And not in Edinburgh."

"Why do you tell lie after lie after lie, my lady?"

"'Tis no lie. Two winters ago, my father took ill and less than a sennight later, was dead." The words stuck in her throat, more so than they did when she spoke of her husband. Criseyde had never wanted to marry and did so only to appease her father. "By spring, the same illness took my husband and many others in Paris. Some fled the city, others remained as I did to tend to their estates and families that remained. Surely you heard such news, even here?"

"I did," he admitted. "And if what you share is true, I am sorry for it."

"'Tis true," she sighed. "I'd not lie about the death of my own father."

"And husband," Sir Hugh added.

"Aye. And husband."

"Then why did you claim he was in Edinburgh?"

"Because I could not share the true purpose of my presence here with you. 'Tis the same story I've told since coming to England, and none have questioned it. None but you," she clarified.

"Your true purpose. . ."

She didn't want to see his face just then, and one look justified her reluctance. "You are pleased with yourself."

"I am."

"And I am tired. Cold. Weary of your suspicions and of being questioned by men."

"Then perhaps you should cease your lies and offer the truth."

Criseyde slowed as they approached a fork ahead. Ranald would know where to ride next. She, however, did not. "The truth is not mine to offer. The truth," she said as her mount obediently stopped when Criseyde reined her in, "could get myself and my companions killed."

Hugh's eyes narrowed. "Yet you've no qualms about putting my cousin and his wife in danger?"

"Here is another truth," Criseyde said, "and the only other one I can give you, Sir Hugh. They were never in danger. I merely sought refuge at Bramton."

"Why attend their wedding feast, cloaked as you were?"

To listen, and learn. To determine if Conall Kerr was a man she could trust with her secret. But that was too much truth for her to offer. "Such cloaks cause little notice at the French court. Had I realized it would bother you so, I'd not have worn it," she said, evading his question. Criseyde indicated the road ahead. "My man, Ranald, is from these parts. He has been guiding our party, and I do not know the way."

"Perhaps if you told me your destination. . . your true destination. . . I could provide more assistance."

"Or perhaps," she countered, "you could allow me to reunite with my companions and be on our way."

His laugh comforted her little. "Until I know whether or not you truly pose a threat to my family, I will be accompanying you, my lady. If you are truly cold, and weary, give me our destination so that we may reach it by nightfall. 'Tis Sutwork, I assume?"

Bastard. Criseyde said nothing.

"Did you intend to be a guest of the baron or do you look to find lodging in the village? It is small, and you'll likely find the only inn full if we do not arrive posthaste."

Lord save her from interfering men. "I know not the baron," she admitted. "Aye, Sutwork is our destination."

"Then let us be on our way." Sir Hugh grinned. "And you will be pleased to know I am acquainted well with the baron of Sutwork. Do hurry. The hour grows late."

Of course he was. Criseyde reluctantly followed, the dreadful man's laughter ruined the moment Sir Hugh of Kenshire spotted her in his cousin's hall. He was all she despised of men and the exact sort her father had warned her about. That he cared so deeply to keep his extended family safe was the arrogant man's only redeeming quality. Besides that, and his visage, there was absolutely naught about Sir Hugh she cared for.

Now she must determine how to escape the blasted man once again.

CHAPTER 8

It was a wonder the woman had made it to the borderlands safely. Her attempts to lose him were paltry at best, and she was the worst liar he'd ever encountered. No sooner had he presented her and her party to the baron and his wife than she was attempting to part ways with him again.

But neither did Hugh wish to remain here. Damned if he'd be the only Waryn man not at that council meeting. Even his cousin Blase, who typically spent his days traveling from tournament to tournament, would be returning home for it, and Blase had much less to prove than he among the Waryn men. In his own family, while Haydn had always been the one who would inherit Kenshire—Holt being the tourney champion like his cousin and Haddie, their sister, the most beloved of them all—Hugh was the brother they called his father's son. The one most like Geoffrey Waryn in his younger years, and none meant that as a compliment.

And yet, if there was one thing more important than his status as a Waryn, it was the safety of his extended family, and that included his Scots cousins. Conall might have been right in dismissing Lady Criseyde as a threat, but Hugh had also been right to question the woman who lied at every turn.

"My husband is dead."

God save him from the next thought he'd had when Criseyde had said that to him. It was not empathy for her circumstance, as it should have been. Instead, he immediately conjured Lady Criseyde with no clothing to speak of. He thought of how her body might feel under the weight of his own. How her lips might feel against his own, how she might taste.

She was a beautiful woman, aye. But more than that, it was the fire within her that attracted Hugh to Lady Criseyde despite the fact that the woman lied more than she offered the truth.

That fire was on full display as he caught her, once again, attempting to leave. Her docile promise that after the evening meal they would have a private discussion should have been a clue. Instead, he'd found her and her companions heading toward the stables where they'd left their mounts not long ago.

"Sir Ranald," he called, approaching them partway through the courtyard. "Do you truly think to leave Sutwork before sunset? After being met with a band of reivers and knowing the terrain ahead? Or did you think to travel west, straight into the Carnwood Mountains? Or perhaps back south, to Bramton once again?"

The man marched toward him, and Hugh welcomed the fight. He'd wondered when the men who were supposed to protect her would attempt to do so. Sir Ranald had unsheathed his sword already, and Hugh did the same.

"You are not my lady's guard nor her protector," the

Frenchman ground out. If he was truly from the border-lands, as Lady Criseyde claimed, he would cease this fight before it began.

"You know these lands, the allegiances that are valued more than any offense I could offer to a woman claiming to be born in Italy, raised in France, and here for a purpose none can ascertain."

"Those claims are true," Sir Ranald said, reaching him. "You will not keep us here."

"You would put your lady's life at risk because she knows not the dangers outside these walls?"

"I would get her away from you," he said, striking so quickly that Hugh was taken by surprise. The man was skilled, more so than he'd expected.

"A crowd gathers," Hugh said, striking back. Indeed, as they traded both barbs and weapons, they began to attract notice. Including that of Lady Criseyde.

"Stop," she called, though neither man obeyed.

Lord Sutwork would no doubt hear of this and inquire upon the fight. But Hugh would pacify him later. For now, 'twas time to end this, which he did easily. The man had been trained at court. Hugh, by both some of the greatest swordsmen in Northumbria and along the border in Scotland. But what allowed him to best the Frenchman was neither of those sets of skills.

Reivers had not the advantage of skilled training, but they did have generations of men before them fighting for their very survival. It was a maneuver the son of Aaren Dunn, one of his father's closest friends, had taught him that saw his sword at the other man's throat.

"Do you yield?" he called for all to hear as he disarmed him.

The other man had no choice.

"I yield," he said, lifting both hands up, including his sword arm.

Hugh stepped back as the crowd cheered. He cared little for their accolades, but wanted just one boon. He turned to Lady Criseyde. "You owe me a discussion," he said, daring Ranald or his companion to disagree.

They did not.

"I APPRECIATE YOU MEETING ME," Hugh said sardonically as Criseyde entered. He'd asked for, and received, a private bedchamber large enough to accept his guest. Thankfully Lord Sutwork was a close ally of theirs, and while he hadn't explained the situation entirely, Hugh offered enough to necessitate this chamber and a reason he and the Frenchman had fought in the lord's courtyard.

"If I had a choice," she said as her maid attempted to enter with her, "I'd be dining in the hall below."

"As your maid will do. Leave us," he said to the woman. "Elizabeth, is it not?"

"It is, my lord," she said, looking between him and Lady Criseyde.

"It would be improper for us to dine here alone," the lady said.

"It would be worse if I were to reveal the true cause of my presence here with you and your companions," he countered. "If you are truly a widow, as you claim—"

"My lady is a widow," the maid spoke up. "But none other know the fact."

Hugh shrugged. "Our host does," he said. "As do the servants, likely."

The lady had been annoyed when she entered the

chamber, but now she was furious. "You had no right to tell him."

"The truth? You give me no reason to do otherwise," he said. "Until then, I will not aid you in your ruse. But please, sit, and share with me the true tale of your journey."

He gave the maid such a look that the woman did not even glance again at her lady to confirm. Instead, she scurried out of the chamber.

"You've scared her," the lady accused.

"Would that I could scare you into the truth as easily," he said, gesturing to the small table. Their host had provided a meal, and wine.

She made a sound of frustration but sat and accepted a goblet of wine from him.

"As I've told you, repeatedly, Sir Hugh—"

"Hugh. I do not dine in my bedchamber with women who use titles."

"Nor do I dine in the bedchamber of men alone." She waved her arms around. "And yet, here we find ourselves."

"Criseyde," he said, realizing it angered her for him to use the lady's given name without permission but not giving a shite, as he really wanted to leave for Kenshire on the morrow, "Do you believe I wish to find myself a guest of Lord Sutwork when my father requested my presence for an important meeting at Kenshire?"

"I do not presume to know your mind," she said. The green velvet of her riding gown had been replaced with another he'd not seen her in yet, he noticed. The deep blue of this gown, also velvet but more ornate, complemented her dark hair, which he'd never seen completely uncovered.

"Then I shall tell you," he said, lifting the still warm bread to his mouth. "I would that I were anywhere but here in this chamber with you."

He'd accused her of lying, but Hugh was not completely truthful in that statement. When she first entered the chamber, he'd reconsidered sending the maid away. But this was no seduction, Hugh reminded himself. It was an interrogation, despite the woman's beauty. And ample bosom, which the current gown she wore did not hide.

"As would I," the lady said, as she took his cue and began to eat.

"Are you a spy for King Philip?" he asked without preamble. From her expression, Hugh's guess was more accurate than he had hoped. "There is no hint of Italian in your accent, which means you may have been born there, but your youth was spent in France, particularly in Paris. The men you travel with were trained by the king's own men—"

"How could you know such a thing?"

Hugh finished chewing his meat pie. "Because finally, after many attempts, I provoked your man into fighting me. 'Tis clear he's more skilled than most, and while I could not have been certain he was one of the king's own men, you just confirmed it. By your own admission, you spent time at the French court, and you are also on a mission, the details of which you have gone to great pains to keep secret. So tell me, Criseyde, what does a French spy want with my cousin?"

For the first time since they'd met, the lady was truly scared, as she should be if his guess was correct. Surely Criseyde realized she would not leave this room without revealing her truth to him.

"Hugh." She shook her head. "I cannot use your given name."

"You can do so easily," he countered. "And just did."

"I've not met a man quite like you before."

43

He lifted his goblet. "Many thanks for the compliment."

"It was not intended to be one."

"But I thank you anyway. You were about to tell me your mission from the king?"

She actually laughed. It was not a sound he had expected to hear this night, but Hugh enjoyed it and wished to make the lady laugh again. But she began to speak first.

"It is rumored," she said, hesitantly, "that the Brotherhood is very sympathetic to the Scots cause."

Of all the things he had expected her to say, that was not one of them.

"It is no secret," he said cautiously, "that the Waryns are married to the Kerrs."

"Which include some who openly support the outlaw William Wallace."

"Not so openly as you would suggest," he countered. "Though I believe it was I who was questioning you."

She opened her mouth for a bite of pie, and Hugh found himself watching for the tip of her tongue to appear. When it did, he had to force himself to look away. His seat, though cushioned, was becoming quickly uncomfortable.

"Your own brother married a woman who defied her own king, did he not?"

Hugh disliked the lady's questions. His eyes narrowed but she continued.

"The Earl of Bramton fought with Edward but reluctantly so. And 'tis said your Scottish cousins, Galien and Boyd Kerr, are some of Wallace's close companions."

"You're well informed," he said. "Though I care little for your questions."

"If you will but answer them, I will reveal my purpose to you."

"You will reveal your purpose to me because you do not

44

wish to find yourself and your companions named as traitors."

"Please." The word was so unexpected, Hugh had no response to it. "I am no threat to your family. Please answer my questions so that I may answer yours."

He looked into her eyes, and unlike so often when they spoke, he saw no guile in them now. But Hugh did not trust his own judgment, not when he'd thought of the woman so often unclothed and in his bed. His brother Haydn had oft said it would be a woman who would fell him, and Hugh began to think Haydn was right.

"What say you of Wallace and his cause?"

He continued to watch her. Criseyde's king bore no love for William Wallace nor any appetite to align himself with those who sought Scotland's freedom from Edward. Neither did he bear any love for the English king, which was why Criseyde's position, and this mission to which she referred, was so dangerous.

He could not predict with any certainty what the lady was doing in England and, more specifically, at Bramton.

"I could find my head on a pike for speaking of such matters in as open a manner as you ask me to do."

"Indeed," she agreed. "You could. As could I."

Neither of them ate, nor drank, nor moved.

"You ask questions I'd be a fool to answer to someone such as you."

"As do you, Hugh."

Dammit. He was as weak as a man could get. Why did his name on her lips mean anything to him?

He could lie. Or refuse to answer. But as she looked at him, something tugged at Hugh which he'd not been expecting. How he could sympathize with this woman after the lies she told, and the merry chase he'd been on with her,

Hugh did not know. And yet, as always, he trusted his own instincts.

"I would support my English, and Scottish, families, above all."

"Meaning?"

"You know well what I mean to say."

She hesitated. But even though he knew her to be a poor liar, Criseyde was certainly intelligent. She would know that there was no path before her but to tell him the truth. The question was, would his Italian-born lady finally offer the actual truth or some other version of one of her lies?

"We may need more wine," she said finally. "If I am to share my tale."

CHAPTER 9

Criseyde's father had only once given her bad advice—to marry Etienne. Her husband had cared more for his position within court than he had for her, and though Criseyde had not expected to marry for love, she'd hoped he would at least offer companionship. But like the man sitting across from her, one she'd seen interact at the wedding feast with many women, her late husband was not the kind of man content with a wife.

Her father knew this, and still he encouraged the marriage.

In every other circumstance, her father had been the wisest man she knew. Kind, giving, and more intelligent than any man alive, he had raised her and loved her well. Criseyde sometimes still refused to believe he was gone.

He'd have been proud of her taking this mission. And would tell her now that if captured by English forces, there would be little chance of getting this message to Wallace. She had two choices now: to hope all she'd learned about the Brotherhood was true and tell Hugh of her mission, or be detained as a spy for the French. He may smile prettily, but she'd seen the warrior too, and Criseyde had no doubt any longer that Hugh would never simply allow her and her companions to leave without knowing if they posed a threat to his family.

In fact, they did not. 'Twas just the opposite.

And so she'd break her vow to the king of France, and hope the decision proved the right one.

"Your goblet is filled," Hugh said, having stoked the fire in the corner of his chamber, "your tale, most welcome."

Criseyde reclined in the high-backed wooden chair, grateful for such comfort, and began further back than likely necessary.

"I was born in Venice to Arcusia Spello and Tommaso di Benvenuto da Pizzano. My mother died in childbirth. My father, a physician, court astrologer, and councillor of the Republic of Venice. When I'd not yet seen ten summers, he accepted an appointment to the court of the king of France as his astrologer and we moved to Paris. Two winters ago, I was wed to King Philip's royal secretary, Etienne du Castel. One year later, both my husband and father were dead as I told you previously. When I tried to collect money from my husband's estate, I was offered instead a lawsuit regarding the recovery of salaries still owed to Etienne. In a judgment that was reached just before I left for England, I was styled "damoiselle" and "widow of Etienne du Castel" but given nothing of the estate. Left with little as the king offered my father and my residence at his court in exchange for his services. I had only what was left me by my father."

"A former councillor and royal astrologer, surely he had an inheritance to pass to you?"

"Aye, a modest one. But I had no official standing at court and no home of which to speak. When the king approached me for this mission, paying handsomely for it, I did not hesitate."

"This mission," Hugh repeatedly carefully, taking a sip of wine. His eyes flickered with the firelight, thoughtful and mistrustful. As they should be.

"To find William Wallace and deliver him a message."

She watched his reaction, waited for something, anything. It was not long in coming. He leaned forward, looked into her eyes, and asked her to repeat herself. She did.

"What message?"

What would it be like to kiss a man such as Hugh Waryn?

That unwelcome thought was followed by another. Some of the women at court claimed that they enjoyed lovemaking with men, though not necessarily their husbands. She'd doubted their claims, having surrendered her desires to more practical ones, but not for the first time she suspected he was one of *those* men.

Pushing aside thoughts that served no purpose, she attempted to answer his question without answering it at all. "That does not concern you. What does is that my mission has naught to do with your family, and so you may safely allow me and my companions to be on our way."

He laughed, a deep, throaty sound that Criseyde enjoyed despite herself.

"I think not, Criseyde."

She should argue his use of her name. Instead, she tried again, knowing she would be unsuccessful. "I was told to give none but the man himself my message. You would have me break a vow to my king?"

"I would have you give me the message so that I might aid you." She'd not been expecting that. "If you truly wish to get a message to Wallace, your instincts, or information, have been accurate. Conall could have aided you, as can I. But first, you must trust me."

It was her turn to laugh. "Trust a man who's done nothing but fight me from the start?"

Hugh smiled, that self-assured, knowing smile that she'd come to know. "Trust a man with instincts that told him you were not simply a wedding guest. Who you know will not simply toss his hands in the air and surrender, who saved you from a band of reivers and who defeated a man I will assume was one of Philip's best. If he truly trusted you to carry a message to Wallace, he'd not have sent you to England, indeed to Scotland, without guards who could protect you." He sat back, clearly pleased with himself, and amended. "Or at least attempt to protect you. Even Philip could not have accounted for me."

Criseyde rolled her eyes. "You have a high opinion of yourself." She tried out the name again. "Hugh."

"I do, until I do not. Go on then, tell me the message."

Though she was unsure what he meant by those cryptic words, Criseyde took a deep breath and repeated Philip's message. "I am to tell Wallace the king will support his cause."

He blinked.

Criseyde was about to learn Hugh's true loyalties. As the son of an English earl, and a powerful one at that, he should be outraged. He should stand, declare her a traitor, and express anger at such a statement. But he did not.

The man that sat across from her was a borderer. Which meant his loyalties were not necessarily with his king. Instead, as she had heard, they seemed to be with his own family first. And that family included the very Scots whom Philip now wished to aid.

"Why?"

That was an easier question to answer.

"As I assume you are aware, Wallace came to France after his loss at Falkirk, asking for Philip's assistance."

"I am aware," he said. And since few knew, at least for certain, of Wallace's journey, that very fact meant something. If indeed Hugh was being truthful.

"He declined to aid him then. The king had no appetite to involve himself in the Scot's bid of freedom from King Edward's grip. But when the English monarch renounced his homage and vowed to fight for Aquitaine, Philip began to see support for the Scots cause as an opportunity."

"To anger Edward."

"Aye."

"And he chose you to bring this information to Wallace?"

Her chin raised. "Why should he not? Because I am a woman?"

Hugh made a dismissive expression that she almost believed. "My mother held Kenshire in her name after my grandfather died, even against claims from her cousin with support from the Earl of Covington." He seemed to realize the name meant little to her. "A very powerful man here in England. She defeated both, and is only one of many women in my family who defy expectations of them. So nay, 'tis not that you are a woman. But here in England, the king has trained royal messengers for many years to carry messages such as the one you do."

"Few believe as you do," she admitted. "And even less here, it seems, than in Paris." Finished with her wine, Criseyde placed it before her only to have Hugh fill it once again. "I am an unlikely choice," she admitted, "but Philip knew I could be trusted as my father was one of his closest advisors. And none, he believed, would question someone such as I to carry such a message to the Scot's outlaw."

"True enough. But if you carry no missive, even if you are able to find Wallace, how do you propose for him to believe you are truly a messenger from Philip?"

"Because," she said, "I carry pieces of their private conversation, one which I will not share as I was told to repeat the words to none but Wallace."

"Were you not told the same about speaking to anyone about your mission?"

"Nay." She shook her head. "I was told to ask questions carefully, use restraint on who to trust to locate Wallace, but for my own life and those of my guards and maid. Philip cares less for the four of us than he does his involvement with Wallace not becoming known until such time 'tis necessary."

Hugh did not seem pleased by that. "You would serve a man with such disregard for your life?"

"I would serve a man with the ability to see I do not starve or find it necessary to resort to. . . other measures as a widow with only a useless title to her name and naught else."

He seemed amused now. "Other measures? Such as?"

"You are no gentleman to ask such a question."

"I never claimed to be."

"Would your esteemed mother be glad to hear it?"

That laugh again. "My esteemed mother knows well she raised two gentlemen and one man with tendencies toward ungentlemanly behavior."

"I do not believe you."

Perhaps she should not have said that. Hugh seemed prepared to prove her wrong. "Would a gentleman tell you that, despite the lies you've told, I am unable to push thoughts of your naked body beneath me from my mind?"

Certainly he did not just say such a thing?

"Would a gentleman greet news that you were not truly married with gladness?"

"Sir Hugh," she reprimanded, ignoring the rapid pace of her heartbeat at his words.

"You have naught to fear, Criseyde. I've never forced a woman to bed me, nor would I conceive of doing such a thing."

"I did not think it," she admitted.

"Good. So now we have but two choices, given the information you shared."

She was fearful to inquire about those choices. But Criseyde did so anyway. "Which are?"

"You could accept my aid in helping to find Wallace, as I know precisely where to find him."

"Nay," she said, sitting up. "You do not know such a thing."

"Indeed," he grinned, "I do. And will miss an important meeting to take you there, but one not as important as the information you carry."

Was it possible he told the truth? Hugh asked that she trust him, but Criseyde did no such thing. She would be a fool to trust a man she did not know, as she trusted few of them she was well acquainted with.

"The second choice?"

"I still take you to Wallace, but first you give in to your curiosity and allow yourself to know what it would be like to make love to me."

She shook her head, about to answer, until Criseyde realized he was not jesting. Neither was she when she said,

"If you were the last man who lived, I'd not make love to you."

"Nay?"

"Nay."

"Liar."

"Scoundrel."

It seemed they were at an impasse. Hugh shrugged. "Very well then. You may bid adieu to the others as we leave for Scotland when the sun rises."

Her mouth opened in shock.

"You did not think I would lead two of your French king's best men, though if that is Philip's best I fear for your country, straight to Wallace. Did you?"

She'd not considered it. "And you do not think I will travel to Scotland with you, alone. A man who just admitted he would make love to me given the chance."

"Come, Criseyde. That is really not so much as an admission. You must know you are a beautiful woman. What man would not wish to make love to you?"

She would not be pleased at the compliment. He offered them, no doubt, like any other words that meant little except to further a means.

"You can't think I will leave my companions?"

"Remain with them here at Sutwork then. You are welcome to ask the baron about Wallace, as he is an ally to the Scots cause. But he will not know where to find him. Few do, and you should count yourself lucky to have stumbled onto someone who can lead you to him."

"I am rarely lucky, and do not trust to have been so this eve."

"The choice is yours, my lady. Either way, I do believe your story and will not follow you. In the morn, I leave, either for Kenshire or the border with you alone."

She stood, unable to think on his words with him looking at her that way.

"I bid you a good eve," she said, unsure what else to say.

"And to you, my lady. I do hope you dream of me, as I will you."

Though he clearly jested, his smile telling her so, as Criseyde walked toward the door she could not help but already see his face clearly in her mind. Of his eyes, which danced with merriment, or his shoulders, which seemed to be as wide as the table at which they sat. Visions of his fight with Ranald, who was truly a skilled swordsman, mingled with the one of Hugh so casually offering his assessment of her.

"Criseyde," he said, just as her hand reached for the door.

She turned to find him now standing. "I will see you in the morn."

CHAPTER 10

Criseyde was mounted and ready to leave, against both Elizabeth's and her guards' wishes, not because she fully trusted Sir Hugh Waryn, and not because he'd saved them from his friends. She followed him now because of how he'd looked at her for one brief moment between arrogant smiles and innuendos. When he spoke of his mother, he was the sort of man she'd wished her husband would have been. The sort she thought existed only in her father and few others.

As their horses' hooves clogged against the stone beneath them, the day warmer than most this time of year but still warranting a heavy cloak and gloves, the man that rode beside her was the one who, though quick with a jest, was slow with assurances that she'd been asking for since dawn.

His one concession? That her companions should travel to Kenshire, where they would be welcomed with his blessing until he and Criseyde returned. Neither Ranald nor Bernard, nor Elizabeth, had wanted her to leave. But Hugh was insistent that he'd take her to Wallace alone or not at all.

"Surely the presence of my maid would not cause Wallace undue concern?"

"As I said, my lady, 'tis your choice. But we go no further if you are unwilling to come with me alone."

She'd not bothered to conjure arguments of modesty, for in truth, as a widow, she had much more freedom now than she had as a maid. Even so, the limitations of being a woman were as pronounced as ever, a source of her continued frustration.

"We will ride through the day," he repeated, "stopping only to relieve ourselves and rest the horses. I would reach the Wild Boar by nightfall."

Criseyde did not lack coin for such a stay, as the king had given her ample for any accommodations necessary. Thus far they'd relied on the hospitality of local lords, monasteries, and abbeys simply because Criseyde had sought those sympathetic to the Scots' cause. Before leaving Paris, she'd been forced to remember all of the names the king's men offered her, since none could be set to parchment.

"You will not tell me where we ride beyond this inn?"

He looked at her as if wondering why she'd asked such a question.

"We could be there sooner but the weather prevents it," he said. The man towered even as he sat mounted. Criseyde sometimes saw him when she closed her eyes. Even now, as they were open, she remembered him fighting with Ranald as if the man had not been the king's champion for many years. Only one man had bested the king's favorite, and that man was the very cousin of the one riding next to her.

"Your cousin, Sir Blase," she said now with naught to do

but speak to him. Criseyde did not care for silence. "He fought Sir Ranald once, two summers past, in Provins."

Hugh seemed pleased to hear it. "It seems Blase and I have more in common than we did before you and your companions came to Bramton."

"How," she asked carefully, "did you do it so easily?"

As expected, Hugh's grin told her that he would not be gracious about this matter.

"My namesake, God rest his soul, was partially responsible," he replied. "My father's uncle. None fought more gracefully or more valiantly than he. Uncle Hugh was trained in the South, while my father by the very reivers you met on the road."

"Reivers are not known in France for their superior swordsmanship."

"But they are known for their fierceness as they fight, like Wallace, for their very survival. 'Tis difficult to teach such a trick, but when you believe your mother or your son or daughter or cousin might forfeit their life if you are not victorious. . ." He shrugged. "'Tis a different way of fighting no man at court can ever learn."

Criseyde adjusted herself on the saddle. She'd not ridden so much in all her life as she had on this journey, but she would not bemoan the fact. "An earl and his sons, trained by reivers." She did not know how to ask the question without giving offense.

"I suppose I should begin at the beginning, as you did last eve. My grandparents were killed by Scots, Kerrs in fact, our home taken from them when my father was a young man. It had belonged to Clan Kerr years before, but like all holdings along the border, Bristol Manor had changed hands many times."

Criseyde was certain she had heard incorrectly. "Did

you say your parents were killed by Kerrs?"

"I did."

"The same clan to which Conall Kerr belongs? The one your family aligns with that they call the Brotherhood?"

"Indeed."

"I do not understand."

"It is a simple enough matter. Bristol was once Waryn, and then Kerr, and then Waryn again. When my family was forced from our home, my father, the eldest sibling, took to reiving to survive. He befriended the late earl of Kenshire, who, upon his death, sent for my father to protect his daughter as she claimed the title of countess. That Lady Sara is my mother."

"Which explains your connection to the reivers," she said. "But not how the Waryns and Kerrs became close allies from bitter enemies."

Hugh's mischievous grin fled as quickly as it appeared. "Halt," he shouted, and she did so without thought. Riding ahead quickly, Hugh disappeared. She was alone on what appeared to be a little-used road. When he reappeared a moment later, Criseyde loosened her grip on the reins.

"A noise ahead," he said. "'Tis but a deer."

He'd reacted so quickly, Criseyde blurted, "You would keep me safe." As soon as the words left her, she willed them back.

"Pardon?"

"'Tis naught," she said, "You were telling me of the Waryns and Kerrs?"

As they came to a fork, Hugh navigated them to the left, away from the Carnwood Mountains. Thankful for the flat grassland in front of them, and also that her hood partially covered her cheeks, which Criseyde was sure were pink with shame, she stared straight ahead and waited.

Thankfully, he made no more mention of her slip when he continued his story.

"That is the most interesting tale of all. When Bristol Manor was attacked, my aunt Catrina accidentally left behind, my father's brother Bryce took captive. And then, with the same charm as all Waryn men possess—"

She forgot her embarrassment and laughed aloud then. "Charm? Do you mean that smile that only a foolish woman who knows nothing of the worth she possesses enjoys?"

The smile she mentioned did not falter. "That is the one," he said.

"You fool no one with it."

"I do not aim to fool but to amuse."

"Oh, I do disagree. I've met many men like you at court."

Now his smile did falter. "You've met none like me, Lady Criseyde, I can offer that vow sincerely."

She believed him but would admit no such sentiment.

"The charm you even now have difficulty resisting," he continued, "proved the beginning of a love match that became only one of many that our two families have witnessed. From foe, to friend, to family, all because of love."

She did laugh then, for the absurdity of the way he said the words. And Hugh laughed with her. There was a part of him, though, that did not mock his aunt and uncle's marriage, but he hid that behind a hood as thick as her own, if not visible.

"That is quite a tale," she admitted.

"Now, 'tis your turn, Lady Criseyde. For we've a long day ahead, and I am not a man who relishes silence."

For once, she could agree with him.

CHAPTER II

S omething was amiss.

When Hugh had come to the Wild Boar, despite its proximity to the border with both English and Scots frequenting it often, he'd rarely witnessed fights within its walls. And yet, it was the first thing that had greeted them.

"Remain here," he told Criseyde, who surprisingly did as he bid.

As he approached, the two men were broken apart, their swords lowered, and the fight over before it began. Magge never allowed weapons inside, and that he'd not been made to surrender his had been Hugh's first indication of trouble.

"Where's Magge?" he demanded of no one in particular, but a young serving maid answered.

"Magge is with God," she said, "not a fortnight past."

She moved along, but Hugh did not. He'd met the innkeeper first when they'd just been boys, he and Haydn accompanying their father to Bristol. Over the years, they had visited on nearly every journey west, and though Hugh did not know a man or woman alive older than Magge, he'd somehow never thought she would die.

The woman seemed to defy death, as inevitable as it was to all others. But of course, it was not inevitable, even for a woman who'd run an inn filled with men who despised each other.

"I thought you'd said 'twas safe here?"

Hugh took Criseyde's arm, not only because it was necessary but also because he wanted to touch her. After learning she was widowed and what her true purpose was here in England, the animosity he held toward her dissipated even if he still did not fully trust the woman. Not only was she not a threat to Conall, but the news she carried, if true, would aid his cousins who trained with Wallace, awaiting a time when they could strike against Edward. The rebels trained in the Ettrick Forest, not far from the border into Scotland. And since Wallace was the most hunted man in England, any discovered with him would be shown no mercy. And that not only included his Kerr cousins, but some of the Waryn men as well. Namely Rory, his Uncle Bryce and Aunt Catrina's son.

"It was," he said as they found an open table. "But the innkeeper has died. I know not who runs the place now, but clearly they do a poor job of it."

How could the woman smell so good after a long day on the road? The scent of lilac was usually too sweet for him, and yet, on her. . .

"You are my wife," he said. "Do you understand?"

She sat across from him, and though they were tucked away in a corner of the great hall, he positioned himself so that Hugh could see the hall in its entirety.

"You said some would know you here. Will they not be aware Sir Hugh Waryn is unwed?"

62

"They will think it but none will dare utter the question. Let them wonder. 'Tis more important to me that none question your position. I'd not have come here if I had known Magge was dead."

"Who is Magge?"

They'd still not been served. Hugh thought of the old woman who, even though she could hardly walk and every bit of her skin was wrinkled, had flirted with his father. It had always amused Holt, who teased their father about it. Her loss would be felt by all.

"She was the innkeeper here for many years. None would dare defy her. Under her watch, that fight would not have occurred. Weapons were always left at the door. And we'd be eating already with ale in hand."

"How would a woman of her age have managed such a thing?"

Hugh thought on that for a moment. How indeed. "I am uncertain in her younger years how Magge established such a reputation, but as a boy I was afraid of her. As a young man, enthralled by how a woman who admitted she knew not how to wield a weapon could hold so much power. As I think on it, perhaps it was because all who knew Magge loved her and none wished to disappoint a woman who'd created this." He waved his arms. "Well before the Brotherhood, this inn has been one of the only places 'tis safe to be both English and Scot."

"Remarkable," she said as the same serving girl who'd told him Magge was dead now brought them a pitcher of ale and two bowls of stew. "Only thing we're servin' after sunset," she said of the stew. "No wine to speak of. Are ye wantin' a room?"

"Aye," Hugh said, "the best you've left for my wife and I."

Her eyes darted to Criseyde. Then, without another word, she turned and muttered something about another Waryn man married.

"She knows you." Criseyde was surprised.

"Nearly every person in this hall knows me."

Criseyde looked about the room, noticing, maybe for the first time, how many people looked their way.

"Everyone?"

"Nearly."

"And yet they do not approach you?"

"If I welcomed them to do so, they would."

Criseyde seemed to notice, for the first time, Hugh looked only at her. He was aware of all that took place beyond their small table, nothing more than a board lying flat across two barrels, but Hugh noticed her more.

"I know that gaze well," she said.

"I am certain that you do, Criseyde."

"I would remind you we are not man and wife in truth."

He laughed, lifting the pewter mug to his lips. "I know it well, my lady, as I've no intention to marry."

"Ever?"

"Ever."

"Why?"

"There is no one woman alive who could sate me," he said. "You seem offended by my words?" Hugh leaned forward. "Perhaps you fancy yourself the exception, Lady Criseyde? Shall we make use of our shared bed this eve and see if perhaps I speak too rashly?"

"You mistake appalled for offended."

"Because I speak only the truth?"

"Because I'd begun to think you were perhaps a better man than most."

"Mmm." He watched her full lips wrap around the rim

of her mug. Hugh would more than welcome a tumble with the beautiful Lady Criseyde of Pizzano. She was the most intriguing woman he'd ever met, her easy acceptance of a mission that saw her from Paris to the borderlands here more admirable than he wished to admit. "A dangerous assumption."

"A wrong assumption, for clearly you are not."

Though her words stung, he'd not dispute them. "You mistake me for my cousin Conall. Or, if you knew him, my older brother, Haydn. Honorable men both."

"But you are not?"

He shrugged. "In some ways, aye. In others, some would question my morality."

With seemingly nothing to say to that, Criseyde began to eat the stew, so he did as well. One thing that had not changed at the Wild Boar was this stew. Delicious and most welcome as they'd eaten little but stale bread this day.

"Today you told me of your childhood. Your father, who you clearly miss dearly. Your writings, which intrigue me." He took a deep swig of ale. "But you said nothing of your late husband."

She did not have to speak the words. That Criseyde spoke so little of him, and from the expression on her face now, he could guess what she would say.

"It was an arranged marriage, the only time my father and I disagreed. But when the sweeping sickness came to France, he insisted. Father knew I would be little protected if he fell ill, the coin he'd collected as the king's astrologer not enough to both house and feed me after he was gone. And so I married." She shrugged. "Etienne was once a notary and was proud to have earned the position as royal secretary. Philip trusted him, but it was the king's favor he curried, not mine."

"Did the man know how to wield a sword?"

Criseyde looked at Hugh as if it were the least interesting question he might have asked. "Nay, he did not."

"We've a word here for such a man. Enfece."

"What does it mean?"

He said this only because it had become clear Criseyde cared little for her late husband. "It means he was likely unable to show you the pleasures between a man and a woman."

By her expression, Hugh knew he was right.

"You are horrid." Though she took a sip of ale, seemingly disgusted, Criseyde's eyes told a different tale. Filled with shock at his words, aye, they were also curious. But he'd pressed too hard tonight.

"Without honor," he agreed.

"None to speak of."

"A wretched man not worthy to clean the dirt from your boots."

She smiled, this game clearly appealing to her. Hugh would depreciate himself all eve to keep her lips upturned in such a way.

"I would toast to such a sentiment," she said, her mug raising.

"And I would toast to you learning someday the true pleasures to be found in a marriage bed." He'd said it teasingly enough that instead of being insulted, Criseyde continued to smile, though she did shake her head.

Perhaps the woman was learning he mostly jested, that he took very little seriously and would not, in fact, dishonor her in any way.

Unfortunately, the same could not be said of the man walking toward them.

CHAPTER 12

"Lord Caxton." Hugh did not stand as the man approached, and it seemed by his scowl it was fully intentional.

"Will you not introduce your lovely wife? I'd not heard yet another Waryn had married."

"Word moves quickly," Hugh responded.

Criseyde hadn't seen this Hugh before. Even when he fought Ranald, his expression had not been this menacing. For a man who smiled often—his straight lips no longer curled upward; his jaw was clenched—Hugh could not have appeared any more intimidating. Unless he stood, which he did now when it became apparent Lord Caxton planned to remain.

"Indeed." The newcomer looked at her. "A pleasure to make your acquaintance, Lady. . ."

If Hugh did not introduce her, or greet this man, there was a reason for it. Instead of providing her name, she looked to Hugh as if deferring to him. Though it was not a game she liked to play, Criseyde knew the rules well.

"What do you want, Caxton?"

If the man had looked displeased when he approached, he was even more so now.

"Your wife's ill manners match your own," he replied.

Hugh stood and took a step toward him. "Say another word of my wife, and Magge's absence will be felt keenly." He placed a hand on the hilt of his sword, his meaning clear.

"You play a dangerous game, Waryn. Your brother's wife refusing her king's bidding, your cousins now lords of Eydington and Bramton. . ." He shrugged. "I worry for your family."

Hugh's harsh laugh drew notice from others around him. "I'd worry for your own, not mine." Hugh's smile was unlike any Criseyde had ever seen from him. "If you insist on feigning worry, do so for your own family. Yours is a dying breed in the borders."

"You'd not say as much if you knew the king's next move." Caxton matched Hugh's sinister smile. "To say he is displeased with your precious Brotherhood of late would be too kind a gesture."

"You would know," Hugh shot back. "You've been licking at his boots for many years. How do they taste?"

Caxton began to draw his sword, but another man behind him held his elbow, preventing it. "Nay," the man, whose colors matched Caxton's, said. "Do not."

Criseyde watched as indecision gripped him. He wanted to lash out at Hugh's comment, but now, surrounded by three of his men, none of whom clearly wished to engage Hugh, Caxton was trapped.

She offered a way out. Standing, she said, "Come, husband. 'Tis late. We should be abed."

If Hugh was surprised by the suggestion in her tone, he did not reveal it. Instead, he glanced her way. Criseyde's hand flew to her bodice. By splaying it over her bare chest, she drew the sort of notice Criseyde intended. All five men stared at her as she shivered. "I am cold," she said, removing her hand and pushing her chest forward, "and wish for some warmth." Though it was clear, by the way she said the word, Criseyde really meant she wished for Hugh to keep her warm.

By now, Caxton's hand had fallen from his sword hilt. Hugh played his part, dismissed all but Criseyde, and came to her side. "I will gladly warm you." His breath in her ear, the suggestion in his tone. . . she could almost believe 'twas real.

And maybe it was. Unfortunately, her body's response to him was real as well.

"I would say well met." Hugh took her arm. "But I am no liar. Good den," he called to the onlookers that gathered. Then, walking forward even though the stairs to the inn's rooms were behind them, he pushed through the crowd.

Every patron seemed to know him, as Hugh claimed. They walked toward the barmaid that had served them, Hugh removing his arm from Criseyde's to fetch the coins, which he gave to the maid. "Our room?" he asked her.

The maid handed him a key. "As you asked for, my lord. All is ready."

He nodded, and they headed toward the front door.

"But if we've a room here, why are we leaving?"

When they got outside, Hugh did not drop her arm. Instead, he headed toward the stables. There, he spoke with a stableboy, who ran instead.

"Our saddlebag," he said by way of explanation. "And I'd not announce to Caxton that we are remaining here for the night."

As he spoke, the stableboy returned. Taking the saddlebag, he then led them to another entrance at the back of the inn, which was, oddly, unlocked. It appeared to be a storage room, though the moonlight revealed little. Exiting the room, Criseyde could hear sounds from the hall to their left, but she and Hugh instead veered right. Up another set of stairs, they found themselves in a corridor. At the end of it, their room, apparently.

Inside, she startled at the large space. "'Tis the biggest room at any inn we've stayed at in England," she admitted.

"Magge added it with coin from my Uncle Neill. His wife was once a barmaid here many, many years ago. He has an affinity for the Wild Boar, more so than even my father."

It appeared more like a chamber that might be found in a castle than an inn. A large canopied bed, a screen with what appeared to be a tub, a private privy behind it.

"The fire is well stoked," she said.

"It would have been started when I asked for this chamber."

"What if," she said, removing her cloak, "someone had been inside here when we arrived?"

"Not possible," he said. "It is for our family's use and none other."

Leaving an empty room at an inn such as this was unheard of. "I think your family is more powerful than I realized."

"The Brotherhood is more powerful," he said, removing his boots. "Together our two families, and other allies, ensure safe passage between England and Scotland. Men like Caxton are an anomaly here. Most like him travel farther west, around the land between Kenshire and Bristol, known by some as the corridor. Or up the coast by boat."

"Men like him?" Criseyde sat on the bed. It was softer

than any she'd stayed on as well, though that was perhaps not so surprising.

"The king's lackeys."

"Loyalists, you mean? Some might say 'tis you who are on the wrong side to fight against your own countrymen."

Hugh poured mugs of ale and handed her one. She hadn't even seen the tray of food and ale when they entered.

"There is but one side here," he said. "Our own. Borderers care little for the politics of the South, though most admittedly care even less about the Scots' bid for independence from Edward."

"It is as if you are a country unto yourself in some ways."

"If such a thing were possible, many would gladly welcome it. The king taxes, takes much, and requires men, but provides little."

"Could you not be arrested for saying such a thing?"

"Aye," he admitted. "Which is why I tread carefully among men such as Caxton. I do wonder what brings him here."

"Who is he?"

Hugh frowned. "His father was once Lord Warden of the Middle March. The man preferred war to peace, taking from both sides of the border to fill his own coffers. The son is as crooked as the father, though thankfully less powerful. But he is a loyalist, as you call them, and has no love for my family."

"Is it so?" she teased. "I could not gather as much from your conversation."

As if remembering that very conversation, Hugh smiled slowly, looking at her bosom without preamble. "A conversation," he said, "which took a most interesting turn. Are you still cold, my lady wife?"

Criseyde gave him a stern look. "I am as cold as I am your wife."

"Even I was fooled," he said. "You did that well, Criseyde."

"I was raised at court," she said. "'Tis all the ladies there know."

"But not you?"

He did not say it mockingly, but almost as if he complimented her.

"Nay, not I," she agreed.

"You are different."

"I thought so once, aye."

"It was not a question."

The way he looked at her was not in jest. Hugh complimented her, and she would accept it with grace.

"I had no mother to guide me. My father was most unconventional. He believed that women were valuable for their thoughts. And I believe it too."

"As do I."

He said it so quickly, so sincerely, that Criseyde could think him genuine. For once, he did not smirk at her as if he would tell a jest. Instead, Hugh simply looked at her, and Criseyde held his gaze.

"You are different too," she said finally.

"Aye," he said, taking a swig of ale. "But for me, 'tis not a boon but a curse."

CHAPTER 13

The bed was hardly large enough for them both.

After their conversation, Hugh finished his ale and left the chamber for Criseyde to prepare for bed. By the time he returned, she was in it with the coverlet to her chin. Her hair, uncovered, was braided and her eyes closed.

Though she was not yet sleeping.

By the time he climbed in next to her, Hugh regretted his promise that he'd remain as far from her as possible. Watching her shoulders rise and fall, he thought of all she'd told him since confessing the truth of her mission.

He thought then of Isolda, how Conall's new wife had also lost her father, though more dramatically, in battle. She too had shown a strength Hugh's mother would be proud of, and he had admired her for it. Had even told Conall if he were ever to marry, it would be to a woman such as that.

But then, he'd dismissed the idea. Marriage to a noble-woman was for Haydn, the brother who would become the next earl of Kenshire. Hugh was glad the title would not go to him. He neither wanted nor deserved it.

"You are awake still?" She turned to face him.

Criseyde had always seemed a formidable force to him, her chin raised. Her stance defiant as she thwarted him at every turn. But now they aided each other, and his fierce royal messenger appeared softer. Vulnerable.

Still beautiful.

"I am," he said, even though the words were not necessary. She could see for herself he was awake, the candlelight beside him and dying embers of a fire he should stoke enough light for them to see each other's faces.

"I never thought to find myself in a bed with a strange man on this journey."

When she lay on her side as she did now, Criseyde's hip was clearly formed beneath the coverlet. She was not slender, her body fully a woman's. He could almost feel the curve just below her waist where that hip began.

Hardening, he agreed with her on one point, at least. "When I spied you in my cousin's hall, neither could I have foreseen lying in a bed at the Wild Boar with you as my wife."

"Word will spread of our arrangement, will it not?"

"Indeed. Which may serve us on our journey."

"But will your family not hear of it?"

"They will, but neither will they believe it. I'm the least likely to marry of any Waryn."

"Because no woman can sate you," she said, quoting his earlier statement.

He amended his reasoning slightly. "I've naught to offer a wife."

"How could you say such a thing? Surely you do not believe that?"

His gaze dropped to where her breasts would lie, not that Hugh could see them. If she pulled the coverlet any higher, her face would be hidden too.

"I've *that*"—he gave her a look that left no doubt to his meaning—"to offer. No respectable Waryn man would leave a woman wanting. Shall I show you?"

For the briefest of seconds, he thought she might say "aye." Instead, Criseyde pursed her lips together as a tutor might to a wayward student.

"I've no doubt you're skilled in that area, but—"

"That you believe so is progress, my dear wife."

Criseyde rolled her eyes.

"You bested one of Philip's personal guards. And easily, if my untrained eye can be trusted."

"I should have said, naught to offer that a noblewoman would covet."

"You mean the earldom?"

"That as well," Hugh admitted. "But more than title or lands. I meant to say. . ." Hugh struggled to find the words. "I've no wish to remain in one place. Traveling from Kenshire to Bristol, to Brockburg, the seat of Clan Kerr to Clave Castle to aid my family where needed. . . to follow a trail with the Dunns by moonlight, borrowing a few sheep for a family who will not survive the winter without them." He stopped, having said enough. "There is no woman alive who would wish for such a life."

"Borrow?" Criseyde smiled. "Do you return them, then?"

"I promised my mother I'd not steal, and so aye, I return them."

"Do you really?"

"Nay, I jested only."

"You do that often."

"Jest?"

"Aye. But I begin to understand the reason for it."

He'd not comment on that. Rather, he would like to return to a previous discussion. "You said, 'I've no doubt you're skilled in that area.' What causes you to say as much?"

"I would rather sleep than explain myself."

"You do not appear tired to me."

"I am not, strangely. Which shows how little I wish to discuss a question you know the answer to already."

"Ahh, you are wrong, my lady wife. I know why I am so skilled, but not why you believe it so."

With a sound of frustration, Criseyde began to turn away from him. Hugh stopped her, his hand gripping her shoulder gently. "Nay," he said, not moving his hand, his thumb stroking the flesh beneath her chemise.

"You said you would not touch me."

"I also told you I was not always an honorable man."

Though his hand remained, it did not move from her covered shoulder. Much as he wished for it to do so, to begin an exploration that would lead to pleasure for them both, he waited. Hugh watched her expression change from doubt to. . . something more.

She wanted him to touch her.

But Criseyde was also a woman who had been with a man who did not give her pleasure, and she likely did not think it possible, even if the feeling between her legs told her otherwise. So much of him wanted to show Criseyde the desire she felt was real, but until she was ready for the lesson. . . he removed his hand.

"We leave at sunrise," he said, closing his eyes and breathing deeply, attempting to forget the curve of her hip.

Forget how easily he could reach out and pull her toward him. With one kiss, he could convince her.

Aye, he was different. But not in the way she meant. Hugh was a different man than her husband, and that knowledge, at least, he could give her.

And would do so by the end of this journey.

CHAPTER 14

"Caxton was nae pleased with ye, Son."

As Hugh waited for Criseyde to come belowstairs so they could be on their way, he'd expected few in the hall, and certainly not this Scotsman who had been sitting alone not far from where Hugh and Criseyde had dined last eve. Hugh immediately joined him.

Gregory Campbell was one of his Uncle Toren's closest friends. Hugh had met him more than once, and while his clan had supported Wallace, they did so more cautiously than Clan Kerr. The Highlander navigated both English and Scottish nobles with a finesse some admired and others found distasteful.

For his part, Hugh held little judgment for the methods Borderland and Highland chieftains used when it came to dealing with King Edward, as long as they did not support him.

"Were you here then, last eve?" Hugh asked.

"I was, but did not see ye in the hall. When I heard what had happened, I looked for ye, but ye and yer wife were gone." The two men exchanged a look. "Ye are not married?"

"Nay, I am not."

Campbell laughed. "You are Waryn for certain, my boy. I willnae ask the reason for the ruse. I thought between Rory getting married and now you, the world was most certainly coming to an end."

If there was another candidate in their family not to have married, it was his cousin Rory. But since he'd found himself properly attached to a wife, it was Hugh who would now carry the family torch as least likely, among the men at least. "Now if Blase marries—"

Campbell whistled. "Willnae happen." Even the Highlander knew of Blase's reputation as a tourney knight, an occupation not conducive to taking a bride.

"I am sorry to learn of your own bride," Hugh said more solemnly. "My father told me just recently."

The look on his face made Hugh regret his earlier words. He'd imagine the same look if either of his parents passed away. Theirs was a love that inspired stories, and apparently Campbell's marriage was a love match as well before his wife passed on.

"A wife is a blessing," he said, "not a curse." But then he smiled again. "If ye find the right one."

"Few of us are as lucky as you to have done so," Hugh said, watching the stairs for his 'wife.'"

"Your parents, your aunts and uncles. From what Alex told me, Galien and your own brother—"

"My family is an exception."

"See it as you will, my boy. Tell me. . ." Campbell lowered his voice even though there were few in the hall so early. "Why were all the tongues wagging about your altercation with Caxton?"

"I'd not name it an altercation. Swords were not drawn."

"Ye'd not have them on your person if Magge were still here, God rest her soul."

"I thought the woman could not die," Hugh said.

"She was as mortal as the rest of us. So tell me of Caxton."

"There's naught to tell. He attempted to goad me, nearly worked, but his companions, and my own," Hugh admitted, "aided in tempering the situation."

Campbell grunted. "Why is he here?"

The very question Hugh had wondered himself. "If he's traveling the corridor, there must be a reason."

"Whatever the reason," Campbell said, "I like it not. I've just left Highgate End. Clan Scott is preparing for another assault come spring."

"As are we," Hugh said. Campbell smiled. "Clan Kerr," he clarified.

"I knew you meant your Scots cousins, but so does Edward. If your family isnae careful, Edward will attempt to take it all."

"All" meant Kenshire. Hugh's parents held it in the king's stead, and only an outcry among all Northumbrian nobles would stop the king if his intent were truly to strip the earldom from his family. They had many allies, aye. And had gathered more, keeping this area of the border safe for travel. But in the end, all men were selfish. It was a lesson he'd learned from the reivers.

"We know it well," Hugh admitted. "You've troubles of your own," he said, no longer wanting to speak of his family's woes. "Will you support the Earl of Carrick openly then?"

"After Edward reinforced Annandale and Galloway,

everything is uncertain. Except the possibility that war will come to Scotland."

Hugh did not doubt it. And courtesy of the woman he escorted north, its scales could be tipped in their favor. But he could not tell Campbell that, of course. The king of France's involvement in the days to come was still to be decided, and if it made Hugh a traitor to his country for being glad of Philip's involvement, then so be it. If England had a king more worthy of the title then perhaps things may be different.

"What is certain," Hugh said as he watched Criseyde descend the stairs, "is that my wife has come to join us."

Campbell turned, whistled lowly, and grinned know-ingly at Hugh, as if he needed his companion to offer his opinion. None alive could look past the woman's beauty, and now that he saw her as an ally, and not foe, it was becoming more and more difficult to do so.

"Good morn," she said.

Campbell did not hide his surprise at her accent. "Intriguing," he said quietly, and then to Criseyde, "Good morn, my lady."

"Sit with us." Hugh stood. "Lady Criseyde, may I present Gregory Campbell of Clan Campbell."

Criseyde sat.

"Pleased to meet ye, my lady."

"You are a Highlander," she said.

"And you, a Frenchwoman."

"Italian," she replied. "Born in Venetia."

"A Scot, an Englishman, and an Italian-bred French-woman. The Wild Boar at its finest," Campbell said. "I would break my fast with ye," he addressed Criseyde, "but I've a man waiting." Then, to Hugh, "A blessing, one such as this. Fare thee well, my boy."

Hugh stood, and shook the Highlander's hand. "Until we meet again."

"As we will, I expect."

Campbell nodded to Criseyde and left as Hugh sat once again.

"What is the blessing he speaks of?" she asked.

Hugh considered lying, or not answering at all. But there had been enough lies between them already. The truth would never steer a man wrong.

"A wife," he said. "Campbell lost his own and said a wife was a blessing, not a curse."

By the way she looked at him, Hugh immediately questioned his decision. Perhaps too much truth was not a good thing after all.

CHAPTER 15

Why Criseyde should care that Hugh dismissed her as a potential wife, she could not begin to understand.

The man was beyond arrogant. Besides, she'd vowed to herself never to wed again, never to be beholden to a man who would just as likely leave her as her father and husband had. Even if she had cared little for the man, with Etienne's death she'd lost her future. And now was re-making one for herself.

Free from a man such as Hugh.

Yet. . . she was no fool. Criseyde could not deny that he provided certainty on a trip that had been fraught with the very opposite. Last eve, in bed, when he'd laid his hand on her arm, Criseyde had not removed it because of the way he looked at her. As he had from the start. His flirtations meant naught to her as the man seemed to toss them around like a noble on horseback riding through town and wishing to garner favor with the locals. But his gazes? Likely he tossed those around as well. And certainly she did not want to marry the man. Even still, the words stung more than they should have.

"Where has the boy gone?" Hugh asked as they stood at the entrance to the stables.

Criseyde looked in every direction but did not see the stableboy anywhere. "Shall we fetch the mounts ourselves?"

"Aye." He pushed open the stable doors and Criseyde followed.

Hugh had looked for him a moment ago to no avail, so they were unsurprised the stables were empty except for horses, their mounts included.

"Is it odd that I should like the smell that others find offensive? 'Tis one of the only memories I have of Italy."

Hugh turned to her as Criseyde paused and breathed in deeply.

"Not odd at all. The stables here are still well-kept at least," he said beside her. "Did you ride then, in Italy, as a girl?"

"I did. Though we lived in Venice, my father often took me to Miele di Sant'Erasmo. His brother is a farmer, and many times I would stay with him and his wife while my father was away."

"Could you not have gone to them? When your husband died?"

As she watched, Hugh leaned against a wooden post, as if he'd not told her moments earlier he wished to be on the road as soon as possible. When she spoke, he listened, and Criseyde was thankful for it.

"I considered it, but a farm in Sant'Erasmo is a different life than the one I imagined for myself. If Philip had not offered so much coin for this mission, I might have been a farmer yet."

Hugh's smile was presumably at the thought of Criseyde as a farmer. "Instead you imagined yourself as the wife of an English knight on a mission to aid the Scots, aye?"

She laughed. "Not precisely, though I've no desire to return to court."

"Do you not?"

She shook her head. "There is naught there for me. The women talk of gowns and illicit affairs but seem to care little that they are treated no better than their husbands' prized stallions."

For a moment it appeared that Hugh might be serious, giving her opinion on the treatment of women careful thought.

"Illicit affairs? Do tell."

She should have known better. "Of course that is the bit you'd wish to discuss." She attempted to move past him, but Hugh stopped her. His hand, like a vise, gripped her arm. When she looked down to their connection, he let her go. The man's strength was unbreakable. And yet, he'd kept his word, sleeping beside her with naught but that one brief touch.

Criseyde had almost wished for more.

"You need not convince me of the merit of the fairer sex."

"As bedmates," she shot back.

"I will not deny it, that I enjoy the company of women. Though if you would but meet my mother, my sister. . . we'd not be having this conversation. I am not like your foppish Frenchmen, Criseyde."

"The mistreatment of women is not reserved for the French alone."

"It is not," he admitted.

CECELIA MECCA

He was not jesting now. No smirk, not even a hint of a smile. Hugh sought her eyes with his own, and though it was like looking into the sun, and she knew that she should not, Criseyde held his gaze.

No words were needed to know he wanted to kiss her. Hugh's gaze dipped to her mouth and Criseyde was not ashamed to admit she had thought about what a kiss from a man such as Hugh would be like.

Would his lips be soft, gliding over her own like those of the courtiers who'd stolen kisses from her? Unlike the marriage act, her peers had not lied about the kissing at least. Some men were quite good at it.

Nay, his lips would not be soft. Like the man, they would be hard and relentless.

When he took a step toward her, Criseyde did not back away. Neither did she give him any indication that she would do so. Curiosity now overwhelming her, Criseyde could almost feel his lips as if the kiss had happened.

Of course, it had not. But it would.

Her lips parted.

Hugh's arm rose, to grasp her perhaps? She would not know, as the stableboy had finally returned.

"Pardon, my lord, a riding party has just arrived. More horses than we can stable."

Her shoulders fell.

As Hugh looked toward the boy, Criseyde closed her eyes. She'd nearly let him kiss her. Nay, another moment and she'd have closed the distance between them herself.

Thankfully, he was gone now, Hugh already aiding the stableboy to fetch their mounts. A good thing, as a kiss between her and the earl's son would lead to naught. Hugh had made clear he did not wish for a wife, and Criseyde had as little desire for another husband. She had even less so for a babe growing in her belly as she made her way back to France.

Just as her resolve strengthened, the very man she'd nearly kissed leaned down to her, his breath on her ear. "We will resume this conversation this eve, my lady wife."

The suggestion in his voice was so unmistakable and arrogantly assured that Criseyde resisted it on principle. "Nay, husband," she said, her chin raising. "We will not."

Hugh's laugh echoed throughout the stables as he led her mare through the door.

CHAPTER 16

"What troubles you?"

They'd been riding all day, a day colder than the ones before it. Each moment that passed, Hugh became more and more angry at a man he never met. As the French king feuded with his own for control of Gascony, Hugh's family avoided such matters while tending to their own.

But as he thought on it more, that King Philip should send Criseyde, a woman with no experience as a messenger who'd never traveled to England before. . . it made little sense. Knowing her as he did now, Hugh did not think Criseyde hid information from him. She truly believed she'd been chosen for the mission because the king had trusted her father and saw her as capable. Which she was, clearly. But why not simply give the message to the men who guarded her?

More importantly, would she have allowed him to kiss her in the stables?

"I've been lamenting," he said. There was no sign of the town they'd hoped to reach by nightfall before them. "Why did King Philip not simply give his message to Ranald or Bernard?"

Criseyde, who had not once complained of the long riding days or their conditions, the hilly slope they'd climbed and descended earlier, frowned. As he expected.

"I do not ask," he continued, "because I think you incapable of such a task, as 'tis clear the opposite is true."

"Then why, pray tell, *do* you ask?"

Hugh opened his mouth to answer, saw Criseyde's expression, and then closed it again. If he gave her the answer he'd first considered, it would be a longer ride to Keston House than he'd anticipated.

"If I were a man, would you have asked the question?"

Hugh thought on the matter. "I'm not certain," he said finally. "It is your lack of experience as a messenger, or someone with knowledge of the Borders, that I question. So aye, perhaps I would have asked it of a man."

"Perhaps. But not certainly so."

"I do not know if I'd have asked the question or not. Does that preclude you from answering it?"

"It should," she said.

He disagreed but Criseyde was unlikely to answer unless he conceded. "Aye, it should."

She was silent a moment longer, the sound of their horses the only one for a time. "He is a deeply distrustful man," she said finally. "My father had been more than a royal astrologer. Philip often asked for his counsel on many matters. Few knew the king as my father had, and with my being raised at court. . . the king is in some ways like a family member to me."

"And yet, you need coin from this mission to live?" He did not hide his disgust with her king for allowing Criseyde to be in this situation.

Criseyde sighed. And then looked at him. "He cares for me, and yet was wroth with me as well."

She was hiding something.

Had he been wrong to begin to trust her? "Criseyde? What have you not told me?"

She bristled at his tone. "There is much you've not told me of your life, but do I take issue with the fact?"

"'Tis a very different matter, as well you know."

"Perhaps."

His eyes narrowed. "Tell me."

"Nay," she said, without thought. "When you speak to me thusly, I will not."

God forgive him, Hugh had little knowledge of how to speak to this woman.

"How should I speak to you then?"

"Gently," she said, seemingly pleased to have found the right word. "As you would your mother or sister. What is her name?"

"Haddie. And I can assure you that if I spoke to you as I did my sister, we would not have found ourselves together on this mission."

"No?"

"No. I'd have teased you, you would have slapped me, and then we would have been scolded as if we were but babes."

She smiled at that, as if he jested. But most assuredly, he did not. His sister Haddie was a hoyden through and through.

"If not gently, then not with anger in your voice."

"Not with. . ." He let out a sound of frustration. "I was not angry before but am becoming so."

"Then we shall speak again when you are calm."

Surely she jested. But nay, it seemed she did not.

Criseyde said no more. She did not look his way. The woman rode as if she knew where she was heading, like the queen of England. Or France. Or wherever she hailed from.

Dammit if he wasn't growing hard, or would have if not for his position on the saddle. He would dearly love to dismount, pull her down from that mare and finish what they'd nearly begun in the stables.

"Do not look at me so."

"Look at you how?" he goaded.

She rolled her eyes. "Philip wished to betroth me to one of his favored lords. I declined. He did not force the marriage upon me but neither did he offer any further aid. I knew of Wallace's visit, of Philip's letter of recommendation for the Scots rebel to his agents in Rome. And so when he began a new quarrel with the English king, thereby changing course on the support Wallace pleaded for in the form of coin and men, I was one of the very few people Philip trusted with the information."

Philip wished to betroth me to one of his favored lords.

A vision of Criseyde under the weight of a man, a new husband who might show her the pleasures to be found between a man and woman, flashed though his mind like an unwelcome guest. He could not banish the thought.

"You are angry because I did not mention it to you before."

Nay, I am angry because I want to be that man, the one poised above you, entering you, watching as your mouth opens in pleasure and your body responds to me.

"Why did you not wish to wed?" he ground out instead. "'Twould seem an easy answer to your problems."

"Easy?" She laughed, the bitterness in the sound telling Hugh how little he truly knew of Criseyde's constitution. "If you think it easy to submit to the whims of a man, to be relegated to nothing but his property, and not even the most valued of it at that, then you are mistaken."

This time, he would not have to force it. Hugh's apology was genuine. "The word was a careless one," he said. "I will think more carefully next time."

Criseyde slowed. Was something amiss? "What is wrong?" he asked.

She continued to stare. At first, her gaze was curious, as if he had said something so remarkable she could not both ride and contemplate it at once. But now, it had turned appreciative with a hint of. . . something more.

"You accuse me of looking at you," he said, "but now you do the same. If we do not ride, we will never reach Keston House by nightfall."

"You said it was not much farther?"

"'Tis the truth. But I did not account for removing you from that horse and taking back my promise not to touch you."

"Oh." She blinked and looked toward the road as if just realizing she had stopped riding.

"I am not certain we should stay as husband and wife this eve," he said, every word a lie. Hugh was very certain that sharing a bed was a bad idea.

"And I am just as certain we should," she said with a grin, spurring her horse forward.

KENSTON HOUSE WAS MORE akin to a tavern with rooms than an inn. Like the Wild Boar, it was a known stop between the borders, and they'd find safe haven here. Wood beams supported an upper floor with candle-lit lanterns hanging from each one. Most of the patrons were deep in their mugs, and Hugh was glad to have found a bed available. Unlike the Wild Boar, the owner here changed often and held less loyalty to the Waryns than Magge had, but Hugh had easily secured them a chamber and bath too. It had been worth the exorbitant coin to see Criseyde's reaction earlier when he'd told her.

Now both freshly washed, Hugh sorely wishing he could have remained in the chamber while Criseyde availed herself of the tub, he and his companion sat for a late supper of pigeon pie. There had been little hint of their earlier flirtations, Criseyde hardly looking at him earlier when he'd bathed. Though he'd left the chamber when she'd bathed, Criseyde could do no such thing. Not in this particular establishment.

And so, she'd turned her back. Hugh watched, waited, hoped she might turn around. But she'd not once peeked or made a move toward him. A pity.

"Tell me of your husband," he said, having ensured none like Lord Caxton graced Kenston House's hall. Hugh knew few of the patrons here this eve, and though unusual, the fact was also most welcome.

It was clearly a subject Criseyde did not wish to speak of. But she did, after a time.

"He was not old," she said. "Neither was he a handsome man or particularly affable. But as my father repeated often, Etienne was well respected at court and in good favor with the king. I'd resisted marrying for many years, and my father began to despair I'd not do so. When I think on it, I wonder if he might have somehow known his time was coming, as Father had never before pushed me into marriage as he did with Etienne."

"Why did you resist marriage?" Hugh continued to eat, the ale as good as any along the border, and for this eve at least, there did not appear to be any threats to speak of. Content to listen to Criseyde's tale, he sat back and waited for her response.

"I'd never met a man that treated me as well as my father."

His mug froze. That was not the answer he'd expected. "Did Etienne?"

Criseyde shook her head. "My father, I fear, was alone in his belief that my thoughts held as much value as his own. He taught me medicine, astrology. . . all that he knew, he shared with me. Though Etienne did not mock me as some men were wont to do, neither did he ask for my thoughts even when discussing matters I was well versed in. But"—she shrugged—"he treaded gently with me in the marriage bed and never struck me."

Treaded gently in the marriage bed. Never struck me.

Criseyde deserved more. All women deserved more. "Men can be cruel. Their thoughts are woven with fears, power, and wealth. . . all poison their minds."

"But not yours?"

He thought on the matter for a moment before answering. "As your father taught you all he knew, my parents did the same. From my own, I learned to fight. I learned loyalty and strength, and I suppose most importantly, to persevere. From my mother I learned kindness and that all things are possible." He held her gaze. "For men and women alike."

"You are a rare man to believe it."

"In my family, I am just one of many who think it so."

Criseyde peered at him over the rim of her mug. Suddenly shy, something he was unused to from her, Hugh was most curious at her thoughts. He did not have to wait long.

"You speak of your family in high regard. But yourself, 'tis not always so."

"I regard myself very highly," he countered.

"I do not speak of your prowess with women, Hugh."

"Do you not?"

She laughed. "Nay. 'Tis plain enough you regard yourself very highly in that."

"With good reason."

"We shall see."

To that, he had no words to offer. Surely he misheard her.

"I have decided to allow you to kiss me," she announced.

Those around them looked over at Hugh's laugh.

"You have decided, have you?"

"Aye."

"And you believe I wish to do such a thing?"

"You've said as much, aye."

She was right, of course. He wished it as badly as he wished for anything. But Hugh also wished to have a bit of fun with his "wife."

"Perhaps I have changed my mind."

"Perhaps." Criseyde took a bite of the pie before her. Hugh watched as her mouth opened and then closed around the pewter spoon. It was the first thing he'd noticed when Hugh first spied Criseyde unhooded. Those lips.

What would they feel like around him?

That was quite different from a simple, chaste kiss.

"Have you kissed a man other than Etienne?" he asked.

"Have you?"

"Kissed a man?"

"Nay, a woman."

"Ahh, yes. I have."

"And yet you are unwed."

"Thankfully so."

"Why should I have never kissed a man while it is plain you've kissed many women before?"

He finally understood. "You cannot deny there are differences between us, Criseyde."

That he was still able to form a thought after she admitted she wished to kiss him was remarkable.

"Less than most believe," she said.

"That may be so, but you've not yet answered my question."

"There is not a woman of age at court who has not kissed a man."

"Were there any that you liked?"

"Hugh!"

He ignored her indignation. "So there were. Think back, wife. Tell me of a time when a man stirred you with his kiss."

"I do not think 'tis a proper conversation."

He took a long swig of ale, refilled his mug, and whispered. "Would discussing the mission we are on, one that could see us both killed were the wrong person to learn of our intentions, be more... proper?"

He should not enjoy the way she lowered her head and looked at him as if daggers would come from her eyes.

But he did.

"There was a man, a chevalier named Jacques le Maingre."

"You did not have to think long on your answer." Hugh disliked the knot in his chest at Criseyde's wistful expression.

"Nay." She smiled. "I did not."

He was finished with this game. "We need more ale."

"He was as handsome as any man. Every woman at court yearned for his attentions."

Where had the serving maid gone?

"The queen did enjoy her balls, and this one was as lavish as any."

"The kiss, Criseyde?"

"Of course. The kiss. All eve he watched me, as he'd done in the days before that night, having returned from battle a sennight before."

"Battle," he muttered. As if a Frenchman knew how to fight.

She ignored him. "I wandered into the gardens—"

"Without an escort?"

"'Tis easier to kiss a man without one, so aye."

"You went to those gardens intending to kiss this. . . chevalier?"

"Shall I tell the story or nay?"

Hugh's intent on asking the question was for Criseyde to recall how a kiss, one she enjoyed, made her feel. To prepare her for the same and to know such a feeling was naught compared to what she should have enjoyed as a wife. But now he simply wished for her to be finished with the tale.

Hugh should have simply showed her instead. "Aye," he said grudgingly.

"Though I'd been expecting him, 'twas a surprise nonetheless when Jacques—"

"You use his given name."

"I kissed the man many times, so aye."

"Many times?"

She frowned. "Shall I continue?"

"Nay."

Criseyde did so anyway. "It was my second kiss and the first time I realized it could be so pleasant."

"I said, nay."

"Aye, you did." She continued to ignore him. Punish him. "He used his tongue, something I had heard was possible but had not yet experienced."

"More ale, if it pleases you," he said when the serving maid finally returned.

"We met in that garden each night we were able."

"Did he touch you anywhere else?"

"Aye."

"Where?"

"Will you tell me every place you touched another woman?"

"You know already." Hugh did not intend his voice to take such a menacing tone. But he cared not for her story. Nor for Jacques le Maingre. "I've been intimate with many women. Surely you'd not wish to hear such tales."

"Nay," she said as he filled her mug. "I would not."

"Nor do I wish to hear more of yours," he said finally, not liking this feeling at all. He knew what it was, even if Hugh had never quite experienced it before. Nay, it was a most wretched thing and another reason he would not take a wife.

"Then perhaps you should not have asked."

"I. . ." He could not explain his reason. "I should not have asked," he agreed. But then had to know one thing. "What happened to your chevalier? Why did you not marry him?"

"Do you marry all of the women you bed?"

"Nay," he admitted. "I do not."

"Neither did I marry the men I kissed."

Men. Multiple men. "But. . ." He stopped. There was no

but. Criseyde wished to prove something to him, and she had, even if he still believed there were more differences between a man and woman than similarities.

"No more talk of kisses," he said. "Not with other people."

Criseyde, who was becoming bolder with every moment they were together, smiled. "Then perhaps we should talk of ours instead."

CHAPTER 17

S he'd never been the boldest woman, but neither had Criseyde been accused of being reticent either. Having made her decision, she would not shy from it or deny that she very much wanted to kiss Sir Hugh Waryn.

But perhaps he was unaccustomed to such forwardness, as the man who claimed to have bedded many women —a claim that nearly altered her thinking on the matter of his kisses—now sat across from her, not hiding his surprise.

"I've heard English maids rarely speak what they are thinking," she said now, pushing the remains of the pie away. "It seems the rumors are true or you would not look at me so."

"If you've heard as much," Hugh said, seemingly recovered, "'tis because you've not met my mother or my sister."

"Tell me more of them," she said.

"They are nearly the same person, one is simply younger and more brazen."

"How old is Lady Haddie?"

"She is ten and nine, though believes she is much older. Admittedly, my father does coddle the woman as if she were still a girl. Nay, a babe. He will weep like one, I think, when she weds."

"Does she have a suitor, then?"

Hugh laughed. "Not one my brothers and I have approved of thus far."

"I would not imagine she needs it to wed?"

"You would imagine wrongly then." Hugh leaned forward. "But I wish to discuss the topic you proposed instead."

"Ahh, our kiss."

"Precisely. Since we are sharing a chamber once again, there seems to be little reason for simply a kiss."

"What do you propose, my lord husband?" Criseyde attempted, and failed, not to smile at his expression. Hugh was like a squire who'd just been told he was ready to become a page.

"I propose we consummate this marriage of ours."

As she expected. "Since I've no wish to return to France with a babe, I will decline your very generous proposal."

"There are ways to prevent a babe," he said, telling Criseyde that which she already knew.

"Perhaps. But it would seem the simplest would be not to consummate our *marriage* at all."

"I disagree."

This was the most absurd conversation she'd ever had with a man. But Criseyde did not wish to stop.

"A kiss alone, or none at all."

"You will not wish to stop at a kiss, Criseyde. I can assure you of it."

"And I can assure you, Hugh, that even the most pleasant of kisses has not, nor will it, make me repeat the horrid act that some so oddly claim to enjoy."

He roared with laughter, so obviously disagreeing with her statement that Criseyde wondered if she could be wrong. There were plenty of ladies who claimed to enjoy it. And though the act itself was brief, so brief it was nearly finished before it had begun, it was not brief enough for her. There was naught enjoyable about it, and Hugh would not convince her otherwise.

"I can assure you their claims are with merit."

"A kiss alone, or none at all."

Hugh leaned forward over the table, his elbows spread wide, his eyes meeting hers. "If you allow me to kiss you, Criseyde, you will wish for more."

"I will not."

"You will. It may not be this eve, or tomorrow, but before I reunite you with your men and maid, you will beg for me to touch you." He lowered his voice. "And when you do, I will gladly agree."

He was so assured, Criseyde nearly forgot for a moment it was she, not Hugh, who held power over her actions. "'Tis a bet you will not win."

"A bet?" He leaned back once again. "I'd not thought of it as one, but will take it. What boon will you ask me to grant?"

She considered it for a moment. "The only boon I wish for is to have bested you, the great Hugh Waryn, son of an earl and friend of the reivers. And you?"

"Mmm, Criseyde. Your request will be my boon."

The way he said the words, Criseyde immediately regretted making such a bet. It was as if she truly did not have power over herself when he was near.

Suddenly, he stood from the table and reached out his hand. There was still ale remaining, but Criseyde left it, took his hand in hers, and shivered as he wrapped his fingers around her own. Hugh's hand was strong, comforting. Powerful and yet still gentle too.

Criseyde said nothing as he guided her through the hall to their chamber. Once inside, she noticed immediately the tub had been removed. And though it was much smaller and less ornate than the room at the Wild Boar, this one holding only a bed, one trunk, and a small table with one chair, a fire was lit already for them.

But Hugh did not seem to notice the fire. The moment he released her hand, closed the door, and locked it, he turned to her. For a man so large, he moved remarkably quickly. Grabbing the back of her neck, Hugh pulled her to him. His lips slammed against hers, immediately opening and demanding she do the same. His tongue swept inside, seeking her own. When Criseyde gave it, he caressed and circled, tilting his head so their mouths might fall more deeply together.

The soft moan that escaped her did so unwillingly. His hand still firmly on her neck, his second one now pressed against her lower back, Hugh did not relent. Over and over he glided his lips over hers.

This was nothing, nothing at all, like her other kisses. It was hard and demanding, but so utterly encompassing that no part of her wished to stop. Indeed, Criseyde wished it would never end. She hadn't remembered putting her arms around his back, but since they were there, she pulled him toward her as if they were not already pressed chest to chest.

Finally she began to anticipate the movement of his lips. When she could feel him harden against her, Criseyde did not back away. Instead, she pressed her hips to him, wanting more, just as he predicted.

When he groaned, deep in his throat, Criseyde wished to break away just for a moment to celebrate her victory. He might be a more skilled lover, but she was giving him pleasure too.

And she wanted to give him more. Hear him make that sound again. And so she continued circling her hips even though it wasn't something she'd ever done before. His hand moved from her neck to her bottom. Criseyde could feel him cupping her even beneath her gown. And then he pressed them together even more, and she could no longer stand. Something within her began to protest, as if she would lose their bet at any moment.

Pulling away, she looked up at him.

He answered her silent question. "Say the words, Criseyde, and I will tear that dress from you and touch every bit of you before we consummate this marriage." He said the word "marriage" mockingly. And though she knew well it was a ruse, Criseyde did not care for the reminder that a marriage, in truth, would never, ever happen.

Not that she wanted to marry him.

But Criseyde did wish for more than a kiss, which was the reason she denied him, as difficult as it was extricating herself from his arms.

"No words are necessary, husband. I am quite content with just a kiss."

Criseyde spun around before he could see the truth in her eyes. It would be days before they reached Wallace and then longer to return to Kenshire. How could she possibly kiss this man and not wish for more?

She sat on the bed, preparing to remove her boots and still not looking at him.

The answer was simple enough. There could be no more kisses.

CHAPTER 18

Hugh would kiss her again by day's end or die in the attempt. But thus far, since their first and only kiss at Kenston House, Criseyde had stubbornly refused to come near him. Hugh knew why, but the reason did not make it any easier to watch her ride. Watch her sleep. Watch her unbraid her hair in the morn or splash water on her face or eat a meal or drink ale.

Every moment they were together, he could feel her breasts against his chest. He could taste her sweet lips and feel her mouth gliding over his. Hugh should have known she would match his passion with a fiery abandon she displayed nearly every other moment of the day. Criseyde battled the elements, long days of riding, and even him with the same resolute intensity that continued to impress him.

But there were moments of vulnerability too.

Small glimpses of weariness, always when she thought he wasn't looking. Criseyde simply wanted to survive in a world not kind to widows, especially those who'd had all but their titles stripped. A title would not feed her or keep her warm at night.

Try as he might, Hugh could hardly imagine how losing a father and husband within a year might affect a person. Even if said husband was so blind that he could not see his wife was a goddamn goddess. Or perhaps he knew but simply could not appreciate the fact. It did not matter. Hugh would right his wrong and convince Criseyde her forced celibacy was no way to live.

Do that and she will lie with other men.

"If we approach Wallace's camp, why do you scowl so?"

"I do not scowl."

"You do."

"If I do, 'tis because we are being watched."

In fact, that was not the reason, but as they spoke, the hairs on his arms suddenly stood straight. Or they would have if he were not so cold. Though he understood, and welcomed, the French's king's desire to get this message immediately to Wallace, sending Criseyde sailing from Paris to Blyth and then across the borderlands in the Month of Wildness was unwise. It told Hugh all he needed to know of the king, and indeed his reputation held strong. He cared for his kingdom and legacy before all else, including the well-being of a woman whose father served him well.

Bastards, all of them. Philip. Etienne. Every one.

"Is that why you continue to scowl?"

"Aye," he lied.

"You do not appear concerned that we are being watched."

"I am not overly so," he admitted as they continued to ride. "It will be Wallace's men, and until they are close enough to see my face, they will follow us north."

"Should you not call out your name?"

"They are too far away still," he said.

The road grew silent except for the crunch of the ground beneath as they rode.

"You said something last eve," Criseyde said. "While you slept."

He knew immediately what it was, and Hugh had no wish to speak of it. But when he said nothing, she continued.

"*Take me.* I woke when you said it first, but then you repeated the phrase three more times. I laid my hand on your chest, and you stopped."

"I'm sorry I slept through it then. You vowed not to touch me again."

"I vowed not to kiss you again. There is a difference."

"If I'd been awake there would not have been."

She sighed. "Will you not be serious for one moment?"

"I am serious," he said, looking through the trees. Still nothing, yet.

"What did it mean?"

What did it mean? That he could not escape that day no matter how often Hugh put the matter from his mind. He thought of his cousin Galien then, how he'd been taken and imprisoned by English soldiers, only escaping with the aid of a woman who was now his wife. The only thing worse than reliving the memory of his own kidnapping was the thought that a member of his family had to endure the same.

"Hugh?"

He would not have told her except for the concern Criseyde showed, her eyes wide and pleading with him to explain. And so, he did.

"I'd been riding with the Roberts clan. You met their leader, Ulric."

"You say it as if we dined together in some great hall. The man threatened to steal from us."

"And would have done so had I not intervened."

Criseyde frowned. "I refuse to believe you rode with such men."

Hugh sighed. 'Twas a difficult matter to explain. "They'd have taken only what they needed. You were not in any danger."

"Taken what they need? Not in danger?"

"Perhaps we should not speak of it." Again he looked to the trees, specifically to a ridge above them to their left. It was from there Hugh could sense Wallace's men.

"I will say nothing, but listen only. Continue, please."

Criseyde grinned as Hugh gave her a doubtful look. "I remember meeting Ulric as a boy, the wildness of him and his companions so instantly appealing to me that it was not long before I begged to ride with them. I was not allowed, of course, until I was much older and made my own decisions. My father owes his life to those men and has told me many times he is not ashamed to see his son ride with them. But my mother does not care for it."

"Do your brothers ride with the reivers as well?"

When he smiled, it was not for the reason Criseyde believed. He'd not expected her to remain silent for long, nor would he wish it. But he did have a question for her as well.

"You mention my brothers but not Haddie. Because she is a woman?"

Criseyde opened her mouth to reply and then promptly closed it. Her features now fixed in frustration, she blurted, "Nay, but because she is so young."

"I was three years younger than she on my first raid." No response. Hugh laughed and continued his tale. "One day—by now I was an honorary member of the Roberts clan—we were besieged by their rivals, another English reiving family. Their leader, a bastard named Ronan, snuck into our camp unheard and unseen. They left two dead, and knowing I was the son of the earl of Kenshire, I was taken with them."

"They. . . kidnapped you?"

It was something he did not care to admit. "I was but ten and seven. Three men overpowered me, and in the melee, it was not until after the fray anyone realized I was gone."

"I am so sorry."

"It was long ago, and I am not that boy any longer."

"But you are," she said. "Or at least, that boy lives inside you. Did this occur during second Jule?"

"It did." He peered at her curiously.

"Did they take you a distance away from where you were attacked?"

"A good enough distance that it took two days to reach their own camp."

"Hmm. As I suspected. My father had a particular interest in that month as it was the same one I was born, and when my mother died. He says Aquarius belongs to the southwest and when the sun is in Aquarius, one can bloodlet or do anything that will last a short time. Quarreling, battling, and holding are neither good nor bad. But of particular interest to you, one should not travel a long way. They were likely cursed and you with them."

"Because they traveled to me?"

"And with you."

"I know some of astrology but not enough for it to influence me."

"And yet, the stars and moon and sun care not what you

believe and influence you much the same. But unlike his colleagues, my father believed men, and women, were not solely ruled by the zodiac. So likely they took you because they are bad men."

Each day this woman surprised and delighted him more than the day before. "Indeed, they were bad men. And still are. My parents paid dearly to have me returned when none, including Ulric, could find their camp. I tried, of course, to escape but could not. My hands and feet were never untied."

"Surely they were when you relieved yourself. Or ate?"

Hugh had no wish to describe either in detail to her. Instead he said, "'Tis many years in the past. I am alive and a stronger man for it."

"What is its significance?"

Hugh hadn't even realized he looked at the axe as he spoke. "I would spare you the details of that tale."

Criseyde did not care for his answer. Before she could ask if he would share the tale if she were a man, he relented, knowing that indeed, he would have. His sheepish grin told her so. "The following spring, my father and Uncle Bryce hunted down Ronan and his men. They would not allow me, nor my brothers, to ride with them. But my father did relent when I asked him to return with the axe. 'Twas Ronan's."

Criseyde stared at it. "Your father and uncle. . . killed them? And brought you their leader's weapon?"

"Aye," he said, silently hoping she'd ask for no more details.

"But. . . do you not think of it each time you look at the weapon? Is it not a reminder?"

"Indeed, a reminder to never be taken unaware again. To be stronger than my enemy."

"Oh, Hugh—"

"Do not feel pity for me, Criseyde. 'Tis not necessary."

"But still you should not have had to endure such a thing."

"Neither should you have had to endure the loss of your husband and father, nor even this journey. Such is the way of life. We endure what we must, learn from it, and carry on."

"I suppose."

"I do not know why I was spared that day while another of my age, Ulric's nephew, was not. But I was spared and am grateful for it."

"Perhaps you were spared to be here," she said, indicating the road ahead. "To be the one to lead me to the rebel that will be the battle cry your Scots cousins need to overcome a tyrant."

She said it with such surety that Hugh could almost believe it. But he had no time to think on the matter, as the very man who may, or may not, help lead the Scots to freedom was the one watching them all along.

"You are reckless as ever, Wallace," he said as three men emerged from the woods to their right. "There are men on the ridge as well, are there not?"

"Indeed. As astute as ever, Waryn. Welcome to Ettrick," Wallace said, looking between him and Criseyde. "Now tell me why you bring a stranger to these woods?"

CHAPTER 19

Though he'd come to court to plead for King Philip's aid, Criseyde had not seen William Wallace before. Few knew he had been at court until he had already left, and fewer knew he'd been there at all. Even so, before Hugh named him, Criseyde knew he was the very man she'd traveled all this way to deliver a message to. He was as large and imposing as rumor named him, but more importantly, there was no doubt this was a man to lead other men.

With broad shoulders and a wild look about him, he was a handsome man, one clearly trained for battles. She'd heard, when not fighting the English, the Scotsman often appeared in good humor, though it seemed to be absent at the moment as he stared at her.

The question of why she'd been brought here was one she could answer easily herself.

"I am Damoiselle Criseyde di Vilardino, daughter of the late Tommaso di Benvenuto and widow of Etienne du Castel."

"The late Tommaso di Benvenuto? King Philip's astrologer is dead?"

"Aye, my father is no longer with us. He told me of meeting you when you were at court."

That she even knew of his visit to Paris immediately made the man less leery. "We met." He frowned. "I asked your father if the stars said aught of Scotland's bid for freedom from the tyrannical English king." He nodded to Hugh. "Your king."

Hugh looked at him as if to say, *He is not mine.*

"Aye, he told me," she said, knowing the Scot would ask about that meeting to secure her claim as his daughter.

"Did he share his answer as well?"

"He did. My father said the Scots' cause would be won but. . ." She trailed off, unable to say the words.

"But?" Hugh prompted.

Criseyde met Wallace's eyes. Did he really wish for her to continue in front of his men? Many, like Hugh, would mostly discount an astrologer's words, but others, like the king, would embrace them so fully as to be dangerous. If they believed her father's prediction, it would not bode well for their leader.

"You are his daughter," Wallace said, his eyes never leaving hers until he finally looked at Hugh. "How does she come to be here with you?"

"'Tis a tale told best by a warm fire. Our journey to come here has been a long one, Lady Criseyde's even longer as she's traveled from Paris with a message for you." Hugh glanced at Wallace's men, the implication clear.

"Any news you bring to me can be shared with them. But come to camp, we will get you by a fire to tell it."

She'd asked Hugh about Wallace's hiding spot but he said she would have to see it herself. As they rode behind him and his men, Criseyde imagined again what sort of camp hid the most wanted man in Scotland and England both.

Criseyde would find out sooner than she realized. Just around the bend, well off any semblance of a road and hidden among the woods, there was a manor house of stone. There was no outer wall or courtyard, naught but the dwelling and a well to speak of.

"Welcome to Ettrick Forest," Wallace said.

"'Tis a manor deep in the woods," she said, never having seen anything like it.

"Precisely so," said one of his men, a Highlander by the sound of him.

"We've just one empty chamber," Wallace said to Hugh, "with all of the men inside until spring."

As they approached, Criseyde could now see a wooden stable behind the manor house.

"We've been traveling as man and wife," Hugh said. "We are accustomed to such accommodations."

"Hugh Waryn with a wife." Wallace laughed. "The idea is as preposterous as Rory Waryn with one."

"And yet Sir Rory is married," Criseyde said, remembering the name from one of Hugh's tales. Both Hugh and Wallace looked at her. She declined to speak any further.

"We've no baths here, no maids to speak of. Just a cook, a cold river, and my men," he explained to her.

"I've had no maid for days," she said. "And am in need only of a privy and some warmth."

They dismounted and a young boy came for their horses.

"We've both," Wallace said, leading them to the front of the manor, where they stepped inside, the darkness enveloping them almost immediately. It was not until they reached a small great hall adorned with wall torches that she could see clearly again. Criseyde gasped.

"We are not the heathens you might think," Wallace said, clearly proud of what he'd done with the aging manor. Tapestries hung on every wall, the rushes clean and all six trestle tables filled. Every man there turned to look at them. Or more precisely, her.

"Do you have a more private place we can speak?" Hugh said, clearly unhappy with something. He had been this way all afternoon, though Criseyde understood easily. She was as frustrated with their situation as he. Even so, she would not give in.

Another kiss like that first one would be her downfall.

"James will show you to the chamber I spoke of. I will be along soon and will have food brought with me. There is a fire burning already. 'Tis my own chamber."

"Nay," Criseyde said. "I will not take it from you."

He looked at her as if contemplating her words but then easily dismissed them. "You will," he said. "Or it shall remain empty during your stay."

She looked at Hugh, who shrugged as if to say, *He will not change his mind.* Already, she liked this man, this leader of other men, who would be so gallant as to give up his bedchamber for her. It was no wonder his reputation was of someone others wished to be near, wished to follow.

"I offer my thanks to you then," she said.

"Show them to my chamber, James," Wallace said to one of the men who'd met them in the forest. "There is someone I must fetch for this meeting."

"Aye, my lord."

As they followed, Criseyde peered back at Wallace and then met Hugh's gaze.

"Aye," Hugh said.

"I'd not asked a question."

"Not aloud, but 'tis the answer to the one in your head."

"How do you do such a thing? How do you know so often what I am thinking?" Indeed she'd been wondering if Wallace was truly as remarkable of a man as he seemed.

"You do not hide your thoughts well," Hugh answered as they climbed a set of stairs. When they reached the top, he stopped and whispered, "Which is how I know you dearly wish to kiss me again even as you avoid it. If you'd but stop fighting it, Criseyde, this could pass for a very pleasant evening."

She slapped his arm, pushing him toward James. Thankfully, with his back to her, Hugh could not see her face. He could not see the yearning in her eyes that must be there, the one he spoke of. Aye, she wished for him to kiss her again. And Criseyde was less and less certain she wished to deny him, deny herself, of the pleasure.

CHAPTER 20

"Who could possibly be inside?"

Hugh no longer had to wonder who Wallace had gone to fetch. Although he did not yet see his face, Boyd's voice was unmistakable. The door to Wallace's bedchamber opened more widely, and sure enough, both the outlaw and Hugh's cousin stepped inside.

"By god's bones." Boyd immediately came to him, nearly crushing him with his embrace. Hugh was not a small man, but every bit of his cousin was pure muscle. His chest, like a rock. His arms, like two blacksmith's vises closing around him. "How does my English cousin find himself here?" Boyd finally let him go.

And found Criseyde.

Looking back and forth between them, his eyes widened.

"His wife, Lady Criseyde," Wallace said.

"Damoiselle, to be precise," Hugh said. At Boyd's expression, "And not my wife in truth." He turned to Wallace. "But I thank you for the introduction."

Wallace pretended to bow. But when he caught Criseyde's eye, Hugh immediately regretted the jest. She was not amused.

Boyd went to her, took Criseyde's hand, and lifted it to his lips. He kissed the back of it with a slight bow. Boyd was as honorable as Hugh was not. His charm was not lost on Criseyde, apparently, as she smiled at him. But Hugh did not begrudge his cousin. Nay, even though he was just two years Boyd's senior, Hugh could only admire the man his Uncle Reid's son had become.

"Criseyde, I would introduce you to Boyd Kerr, son of Reid and Allie of Clan Kerr."

"You are Hugh's cousin."

"Through marriage, aye. My father is the brother of Catrina Kerr, who is married to Hugh's Uncle Bryce."

"I will need to put all these names to parchment," she said as Boyd dropped her hand. "Your family," she said to Hugh, "is quite large."

The corners of his lips tugged up. "Indeed, it is larger than many."

Criseyde rolled her eyes at him. Though she'd kept herself apart from him these past days, Hugh sensed a shift in her today and meant to exploit it.

"I am glad," Boyd said, "you do not take offense to my cousin's crude humor. I fear he's spent too much time amongst the reivers."

"And you have clearly spent too much time with my mother," Hugh countered. "For your words could have come from her mouth."

Wallace indicated that they should sit. As promised, he'd sent food and ale to the chamber. A table large enough for six people served as a meeting place for a small group of men, and Hugh had been in the very seat where he sat now more than once before.

After Falkirk, Wallace's men had discovered this abandoned manor house in the woods, likely once a signal tower as evidenced by the iron basket that was discovered on its summit. Though Hugh could understand why it had been abandoned. Getting supplies here had been a problem since the start.

"You will see," Wallace said to Criseyde, "they fight each other like the devil fights the light, until one of their own is threatened. When that happens," he crossed himself, "God save the man or woman who would bear the brunt of it."

Boyd, who sat next to Criseyde, poured her wine. "We serve ourselves here," Boyd said. "There are no maids or other servants, just the men and a cook."

"As I've told Sir William, I've been without a maid for many days." She reached for a piece of bread.

"Though she has come from the French court," Hugh said proudly, "Lady Criseyde has adapted easily to the life of a royal messenger." He was rewarded for the compliment with a smile. Hugh smiled back.

"Not man and wife in truth then?" Boyd asked, his implication clear.

As each of them filled their plates, Wallace finally asked the question they'd come here to answer. "Tell us, then, why are you here?"

The men looked at Hugh, but this was not his tale to tell. "Criseyde?"

As she began to speak, Hugh watched as she transformed from his companion to a woman who clearly had been raised at court. He could almost forget the woman who abandoned herself to his kiss. Who had challenged him earlier that day to a race. Who had intervened with him and Caxton at the Wild Boar.

Transfixed, he heard her speak but had to focus to truly hear her words.

"He has changed his thinking on your request. King Philip would supply you with both coin and men, despite his earlier denial."

Though Wallace had no reaction, his cousin's eyes widened in surprise. "He was adamant that he could not do so."

Boyd, as much as any of his clan with the exception of perhaps Galien, was embedded in Wallace's camp. He'd fought in every battle with him despite his father's plea otherwise. Clan Kerr wished for Scotland's freedom, but they were not yet decided on who to support with so many claimants to the throne. Boyd argued, rightly so, that Wallace was not one of those men who coveted the crown for himself. The man simply wished, as many of them did, to be free of Edward's clutches.

"He wishes to punish Longshanks for the renewed fight in Gascony?" Wallace guessed.

"And Philip knows the English king prepares to fight for Aquitaine."

That surprised Wallace. "Even in England that is not common knowledge."

"My king is shrewd," Criseyde said.

"Shrewd enough to know the winds of power are changing." Boyd's jaw clenched as it did when he became angry. "And when they change again?"

"That is for Sir William to decide. I am simply here to share the message and let you," Criseyde turned toward Wallace, "decide. If you accept the king's offer, I have instructions as well along with them."

"Instructions that could put my men in danger?"

"Instructions on how to proceed," she said, taking a sip of ale.

"Tell me," he said.

The room grew quiet. All four of them continued to eat. Criseyde finished chewing and answered. "On the last day of Hocktide, he will send coin and an envoy to Gurstelle Cove. There he will send further instructions, at your will."

Wallace, rightfully suspicious, looked at Hugh. "This could be a trap?"

Of course Hugh had thought so as well. Even after he'd left her companions behind, there were times when he wondered if Criseyde could be playing him, and Wallace, false. But he had to trust his own instincts, and Hugh had been with Criseyde long enough to form an opinion of her.

"It is not," he said, his tone firm.

He met Criseyde's eyes.

"How many men?" Boyd asked.

Criseyde had never offered the details of King Philip's offer to him. She'd told Hugh that message was for Wallace directly.

"He can provide thirteen hundred men-at-arms and two hundred and fifty cross bowmen."

Boyd whistled. "That could turn the tide back in our favor," he said to Wallace.

"If it is true, aye."

Wallace had not won so many battles by being rash. He was a trained knight, a skilled warrior, and had much experience in planning for war. The battle for Stirling was, of course, unfortunate, but Wallace had not come here to hide. His men continued to train, and come spring, there would be tents outside these walls as far as one could see.

"It is true," Criseyde said. "I give my vow to you as Sir

Hugh's wife." She smiled. "I share only the words King Philip offered to me."

"And you believed him?" Wallace asked.

"He has not lied to me, or to my father, who served him well for many years. There is much I do not agree with him about, but the king has never dishonored me, my father, or my husband."

"Husband?" That, from Boyd.

"She is a widow," Hugh explained.

Boyd raised his mug to the group. "We know not how you came to meet my cousin or how you found yourself 'married to him' for this journey, but you are most welcome here, Lady Criseyde. As your king's men are most welcome come spring on the shores of Scotland."

Wallace lifted his mug as well. "Aye, they are most welcome indeed. Thank you for carrying this message to me."

Both Hugh and Criseyde lifted their mugs.

"Bas Agus Buaidh," Wallace said.

"Victory or death," Hugh repeated for Criseyde's benefit.

Their mugs clinked together, the wheels of the next major battle in Scotland's bid for freedom clogging forward this eve. But there was just one thought on Hugh's mind, and it had naught to do with victory or death or battles or any damned kings.

It was simply a woman's kiss he thought of, and that very woman, if his guess was correct, was thinking the same thing.

CHAPTER 21

"I will show you to the guardhouse," Boyd said to Hugh after Wallace left.

Criseyde, who had been stoking the fire at his words, froze. With her back to them, she could not see either man's face. She didn't want Hugh to leave but certainly could not say as much.

"I will remain here," Hugh said, his tone broking no argument. "You know these men, but I do not. And though I am certain all those in Wallace's personal guard are honorable, I would not risk Criseyde to be certain."

"None would dare to harm her," Boyd said.

Criseyde would not leave the results of this decision to the stars. She turned, meeting Hugh's eyes. Startling at the look he gave her, full of promise, Criseyde had difficulty looking away. But she did and turned to Boyd.

"Your cousin has protected me well on this journey, and I would rest easier if he continued to do so."

They'd told Wallace and Boyd their tale, so Criseyde was unsurprised at Boyd's smile. "After a time, of course."

She returned his smile with one of her own. "After a

time," Criseyde agreed. "Before I told him my story, Hugh did not relent. King Philip and his men prepared me to answer questions. They prepared me to stay hidden until I could find a way to Wallace. But they did not prepare me for Hugh Waryn."

Boyd laid his hand on Hugh's shoulder. "When we were but lads, Hugh and his brother Holt came to Bristol Manor."

"Bryce and Catrina's home," Hugh reminded her after Criseyde admitted difficulty in remembering all of the connections in his family.

"That is one I remember easily," she said. "'Tis difficult to forget a love story that began with. . ." She stopped.

"Kidnapping," Hugh said. "You need not shy from the word."

"You told her?" Boyd seemed surprised by the fact.

"I did."

Boyd looked more closely at Criseyde, as if seeing her for the first time. Under his gaze, Criseyde did not flinch. But she did feel as if she were exposed, like Boyd knew something of her she did not.

He took his hand from Hugh's shoulder. "Holt," he said, continuing his tale, "had been a good rider even then. The boy was always poised to become a man who could unseat anyone in the kingdom with a lance."

"Even I have heard the name Sir Holt in France. He and Sir Blase are two of the Englishmen we know well, though I'd not realized they hailed from the same family."

"Indeed, the two have trained together since they were lads. On that day, young Holt had been showing some of the maids his tricks."

"He stood on his horse's back," Hugh said. "Mother hated to see it. Still does, in fact."

"I had asked Hugh to train with me, but he refused to

leave Holt. After a time, the trick had become tiresome to all but Holt and one maid in particular. I asked Hugh again to come to the training yard with me, but he still refused."

"If I'd left Holt alone while he performed that particular trick, my mother would have sensed it from Kenshire and come for both of us."

"You protected him," Criseyde realized. "Though what protection could you offer if he had fallen?"

"I will tell you," Boyd said. "None but his brother saw anything untoward. But as Hugh suddenly ran toward his brother, I could see finally what he'd spotted earlier. Though patient and well-trained, Holt's mount had decided he no longer wished to have a form towering above him."

Criseyde's eyes widened. If his horse became skittish with him standing on its back. . . "He could have easily been killed. His neck, broken."

"Aye, but he did not. Hugh ran to him, took the mount's reins in his hands, and steadied him. Holt dismounted but still the horse did not calm. It surprised Holt most of all, as he'd trained the horse himself."

"Hugh saved his brother's life."

"Possibly, aye. And taught him a lesson that day as well."

"Not to use tricks to woo women?"

Hugh laughed. "My brother does that even now. Nay, Holt needed to learn a measure of caution that was absent in him before that."

"But have you learned it yourself?" she asked.

Boyd's laughter followed him to the door. "She knows you well, cousin. I will leave you to your sleep. We'll speak more in the morning."

"Aye," Hugh said. "We've much to discuss."

Boyd grinned, and with a quick glance at Criseyde, he said, "We do." His meaning was clear. They would speak of her. But what would Hugh say?

"Good eve, my lady."

"Criseyde," she said, giving Hugh's cousin leave to use her given name.

"Boyd." He nodded to Hugh. "I am glad to have you here, if for but a day."

They'd agreed to remain as Wallace's guests to rest tomorrow before leaving for Kenshire, a longer journey than from Bramton.

"As am I." But when Boyd left, Criseyde realized it was not Boyd he spoke to when saying those words. He said them, instead, to her.

"I am pleased with Wallace's acceptance of me," she said as Hugh locked the door. "Philip said 'twould be as challenging to do so as finding a man who did not wish to be found. He offered many different days to rendezvous depending on when, or if, I found him. In truth, he never expected for the Hocktide meeting to occur."

"Coming to Bramton was wise," he said. "Did Philip counsel you to do so?"

"He counseled me to seek out any member of Clan Kerr. I was given leave to tell them of my plan. When I learned Conall was nearby, I went to the priest there."

"It could have been dangerous, this mission of yours."

"If not for you. I found Wallace because of you. He accepted my tale easily because of you."

He took a step toward her.

"Do you realize what you've accomplished here today?" he asked.

"What we accomplished." Criseyde closed the distance between them. "I was afraid," she said, stopping so close to him she could reach her hand out and touch him if she wished.

"History will know your name if Wallace is successful. I will make certain of it." His smile was not triumphant but full of resolve.

"That is all well, and I am happy to have delivered the message. But now, I wish only for you to kiss me again."

As if he'd been waiting for that very request, Hugh closed the remaining space between them. He pulled Criseyde into his arms, and just as she was engulfed by the warm embrace, Hugh captured her lips with his own. They glided over hers with a need she understood. When their tongues touched, days of repressed desire were unleashed.

His hands lowered from her back to Criseyde's buttocks, squeezing through her gown until he quickly removed them, breaking their kiss and cursing. "My apologies. A kiss only."

She'd liked the feel of his hands on her and wished for it again. But if she asked, Criseyde would have lost. He waited for her response, his lips still glistening from their kiss. She wanted more, but Criseyde had been losing to men her whole life.

"A temporary stay," he said. "This one night. From our bet."

"If I conceded—"

"You conceded nothing, Criseyde. It is I who wishes to kiss you, to touch you. Tomorrow we will begin the bet anew."

Perhaps if she did not say the words. . .

Criseyde nodded.

Hugh took her in his arms again, but this time, as his lips found hers, he reached behind her back. As if he'd done it many, many times, Hugh unlaced her gown while he continued to move his tongue expertly across her own.

The ease with which Hugh removed her gown should have given her pause. Instead, she returned his kisses greedily, and not knowing precisely what she was doing, Criseyde attempted to pull his tunic from him. Hugh aided her, never breaking contact with her, and did the same with his shirt. He only tore himself away to lift the linen shirt over his head.

Criseyde gaped at the sight before her. "Your chest," she said foolishly. "And arms." Criseyde ran her fingers along the muscles, knowing not all knights were similarly formed. "'Tis perfect," she said.

"Not as perfect as you." Hugh then reached down to remove his boots and Criseyde did the same. Where they'd been frantic earlier, now their movements were slow, neither breaking eye contact as their boots were tossed to the side. Criseyde would have stopped there, but Hugh continued to undress. It was a one-night stay. If not tonight, then never. Tomorrow they would once again be messenger and guide.

Nay, protector.

Criseyde may not want to need one, but she could not deny enjoying Hugh's presence these past days.

"If you remove that shift," he said, "I will do more than simply touch you this night."

Criseyde hesitated but then grabbed its hem and lifted the garment above her head. When she was finished, Hugh's expression was not her only surprise. He had fully undressed as well, and though she'd seen her husband and thought she was fully prepared, Criseyde was not.

"Hugh," she began, when he stopped her. Came to her.

"Let me show you, Criseyde. Let me show you how it should have been."

The way he looked at her body, the feeling inside her stomach as his hands ran over her hips, upward, Hugh's palms touching her breasts briefly as they continued to move toward her cheeks. . .

"I will trust you," she said, "as you trusted me."

"But still do not believe you will find pleasure in this?"

She shook her head. "Neither do I wish for a babe and no husband to aid in its caring."

"I will not spill my seed in you, Criseyde." He reached down to cup her breasts in both hands. Then, leaning his head down, he kissed one of them. His tongue swirled around her nipple before he took it into his mouth, suckling. Criseyde clenched, the feeling extremely pleasant. Hugh did the same to her other breast and then smiled, knowingly. "But I will show you."

Criseyde could not ask precisely what he'd show her, for his lips were once again on hers. As he kissed her, Hugh's hand found its way to her thigh. It was not until his palm rested between her legs that she realized his intent.

And then his finger was there. She gasped as it entered her.

"He did not do this to you?"

Then another finger.

Criseyde shook her head. "You are angry."

"Not with you," he said, his features softening.

And then, they moved. A jolt ran through her as his thumb rubbed her as well. Criseyde gripped his shoulder with her fingers. Hugh smiled, but she could not. Criseyde could do nothing but feel as his fingers circled, pushing in and out. Each time his thumb touched her she thought she might collapse onto the ground.

"Hugh," she breathed. Criseyde wanted more, but suddenly, his fingers were gone. He reached onto the nearby table, grabbed a cloth, and then lifted her so easily into the air Criseyde could not form a thought. Her back touched the cool coverlet beneath her, and Hugh climbed above her. They were on the bed, Criseyde in a position she'd been fewer times than other wives, if they were to be believed.

But never had her husband looked as Hugh did, towering above her. Neither had he ever made her feel as he had just then when he'd touched her.

Spreading her legs, Hugh leaned down and kissed her again. Nearly made her forget until. . . he was there. About to be inside her. He stilled, waiting. When she realized he waited for her, Criseyde kissed him harder.

He pushed into her.

From the start, it was different. He glided in easily, and there was no pain at all. In fact, as he began to move, Criseyde found herself moving with him. With each thrust of his tongue, his hips circled in the same way.

When he touched her again, his hand between them, Criseyde jolted her hips upward. Her buttocks squeezed as she began to pulse. She never wanted it to stop. Again and again she rose off the bed to meet his thrusts until Criseyde could not help but whimper.

"Please," she begged.

Hugh lifted his head.

His thumb circled her as Hugh pumped into her, slow and circling and then faster. Her heart would surely burst at the pleasure of it, of his expression as he watched her. There was pleasure for him too, and the knowledge of it. . . she stopped resisting.

With a final squeeze she burst, unable to think. Unable

to do anything but be aware of the fullness of him. It continued, and finally, she squeezed her eyes shut. With a sound very much like a growl, Hugh pulled himself from her. When she opened her eyes, they widened.

He was above her, kneeling, a cloth wrapped around him. But it was his expression she watched as his own eyes opened. Moving the cloth over him, he then jumped from the bed. With Hugh's back to her, she couldn't see what he was doing at the high table, but she did hear a splash of water from the bowl that was left for them to clean with.

Criseyde's head dropped. Her legs still spread, she had no will to move them. Or even to open her eyes, which she only did when she sensed Hugh standing above her.

He sat beside her, the silent question between them.

"You were right," she said. "And now. . . I understand."

CHAPTER 22

He couldn't sleep.

Usually when Hugh had difficulty sleeping, it was the night before a battle. Otherwise, his mother was fond of saying a trebuchet could launch a boulder into his bedchamber and Hugh would sleep through it.

Yet the only battle he would fight in the morn was the same one he had all eve since Criseyde fell asleep. After making love for the second time, Hugh not willing to waste the one-night stay she'd granted them, she had drifted off in his arms, where she lay still.

And though they'd traveled hard to get to Wallace's camp, still sleep eluded him. Hugh could not stop thinking of the moment Criseyde first found pleasure.

He smiled into the dark.

More precisely, when he'd helped her find it. When he closed his eyes now, it was her expression he saw. Criseyde could not have been more surprised telling him what he already knew. Her husband had neglected her in the bedchamber. He simply could not understand it. What man

133

could look at Criseyde for more than a moment and do such a thing?

A man who resented her forward thinking, perhaps? One who felt threatened by her intellect? For there was no other possible reason. The woman was damn near perfect. Her only flaw? That she seemed to somehow see through him. And Criseyde was not shy in telling Hugh precisely what she thought of him.

I need to sleep.

And yet, Criseyde was no longer lying in the crook of his arm. She was draped on him, her leg slung around his. The coverlet only partially on them. Hugh blinked and then opened his eyes. It seemed he had fallen asleep after all, as sunlight streamed into their chamber from a small arrowslit.

When she stirred, Hugh resisted pulling her atop him, waking Criseyde fully, and repeating the night before. There were complications to that particular plan. First, Criseyde's stubbornness, which would not allow her to admit defeat, though he knew well it was about more than a silly bet. And second, Hugh had undeniably never, not once in his short life, experienced the sort of tug on his chest he'd felt when Criseyde had found release.

Pleasure? Aye. A fondness for the woman he'd been with that had made him wish to repeat the act again? He'd had that too, though not as often. But nothing like being with Criseyde, and frankly, he could not fall into the same trap as Conall or his brother. Since his kidnapping, Hugh had been asking himself why he had been spared. What, precisely, was his purpose as the second son of Geoffrey Waryn? He could not possibly take a wife. Who would wish to be with a man who wandered from England to Scotland, from his home to his family's holding, searching for a reason to be useful? Neither would Criseyde ever wish to become a wife again, and Hugh could not blame her for a moment, not after the way she'd been treated by her first husband.

"Is it time to rise, then?"

If he turned, she would see he'd already fully risen. Instead, he remained with his back to her, stoking the fire.

"I thought to seek out Boyd to speak with him. Will you come with me? I'd prefer not to leave you alone here."

Taking a few deep breaths, he was finally ready to dress and did so without once looking at Criseyde. He heard her moving about and only looked at her once he was certain she had already dressed. "Shall we go then? I will ask for fresh water," he said, handing her a sprig of mint to chew. "Is there aught else you need?"

She had just two gowns with her, and though Hugh was well used to seeing her in both, he was not accustomed to looking at Criseyde after they'd made love, twice. He thought of the second time, Criseyde knowing full well what was to come. But still, he had not wished to move quickly, as it would be their last time together. He'd flipped them so Criseyde was atop him, and had not been surprised she enjoyed being able to set their pace.

He reached for his sword, sheathed it, and opened the door without another glance. He simply could not calm himself this morn. Thankfully, voices from the hall saved him from dwelling on the memory of Criseyde's breasts bouncing with each thrust of his hips. She'd smiled at him before tossing her head back and moaning as Hugh used his thumb to ensure her pleasure.

Stop.

Wallace's men were already breaking their fast, most nearly finished with their meals, but the voices they'd heard earlier ceased the moment Criseyde walked into the hall. At first, Hugh thought it was because they'd been here without a woman to speak of. But as the men began to clap, Hugh realized Wallace must have spoken to them.

There was no head table. Wallace stood at the end of the room and gestured for them to join him. Boyd sat next to him with two other men, the bench across from the four men occupied by two others. Hugh sat, allowing Criseyde to do so on the end of the bench with ease.

"You told the men," Hugh said as they sat.

The meal was sparse, just bread, broth, and ale.

"They were curious to learn about the beautiful guest and Sir Hugh's companion," Wallace said. "And sorely needed good tidings."

"I thank you for the kind words," Criseyde said next to him. Hugh still had not looked properly at her this morn, but he did so now. Beautiful indeed. Immediately he thought of her above him, her head tossed back, calling his name.

This would not do.

"We've still much to discuss." Boyd reached for more ale. "You've not told me of Conall yet."

Though they'd just sat down, Wallace slapped his cousin on the back and stood. "I will leave you to your reunion. Come," he said to the other men, who were also finished with their meal. "If your sword arm needs practice, I will gladly match skills against the great son of Geoffrey Waryn since I cannot best his cousin."

"None here have done so," Boyd admitted, but Hugh was unsurprised.

"You will find me less skilled than he but enough to best you easily," Hugh said, smiling.

"I look forward to proving you wrong, Waryn. My lady."

Wallace nodded to Criseyde in parting.

When the men left, Hugh peeked again at Criseyde. Her head was bent as she took a sip of broth but she sensed his notice. Just as she opened her mouth, Hugh looked away. When he once again caught his cousin's eyes, Boyd was watching him carefully.

"I've been here, at Wallace's camp, since the battle, but have heard rumors. Tell me."

Hugh thought back to the beginning. "You know of Conall's vow to the Earl of Bramton at Pexford." Since Stirling, King Edward had been celebrating his victory over Wallace by continuing to press north of the border. His aim, to quell further uprisings. Thankfully, the Scots had warning that Edward's men would strike at Pexford and were prepared. The battle was easily won, the king's men retreating nearly as soon as they struck. Hugh had been there, as had his cousins Conall and Boyd, as well as Conall's father, Alex Kerr.

"I knew he'd made the vow but still was surprised he actually married the woman."

"As was Conall. When he arrived at Bramton, Lady Isolda did not believe his tale. And she was betrothed already."

Though Boyd appeared confused, Criseyde was not. He'd told her this story, and many others of their family, on this journey. She had said little this morn, and Hugh wanted to ask her if anything was amiss. But he did not dare.

He was no fool. Hugh was falling in love with a woman who would soon rejoin her men and return to France. It was no wonder he seemed so tormented.

"Why would the earl wrest a vow from Conall to marry his daughter if she was bound to another already?"

None knew for certain since the earl died on the battle-field that day, but they could guess. "Isolda, and her mother, believe that when he was betrayed, killed on that field by his own men, he realized Isolda needed someone with more strength, and connection, than the whelp of a man she was promised to. I met him, unfortunately, and am not certain why the earl agreed to the match at all."

"Why does any father promise his daughter to such men?" They both looked at Criseyde, Hugh understanding but Boyd not. "I did not care for my husband," she said by way of explanation. "But will not speak ill of the dead."

"Did he hurt you?" Boyd asked.

Criseyde, seemingly surprised by his cousin's direct-ness, thought on that for a moment. "I would have said nay before. . ." She stopped.

Before she met him. Hugh's teeth ground together. Not for the first time he was glad the Frenchman was already dead, as he would have gladly seen it done otherwise.

"He did not beat me," she finished. "I do apologize for interrupting your story."

Their eyes met. Hugh was sorry for the way she'd been mishandled in her marriage, and he was sorry for mishan-dling her now. In some ways he was as big a fool as her damned husband.

"Lady Isolda was betrothed," Boyd said. "And did not believe her father wished for Conall and she to wed. And yet, they are man and wife."

Hugh had not planned to tell the tale this way. There was much more to the story, from Isolda's betrothed arriving at Bramton to her being taken by the marshal who had been undermining the earl all along. Instead he said simply, "They fell in love."

He would not, could not, look at her.

Boyd's brows furrowed. "There is more to the tale, I can see it in your eyes."

"There is," he agreed. "But I do not wish to bore Criseyde with it, as the story is one she's heard already."

"I have not once been bored in your company."

Again, their eyes met and locked. Boyd cleared his throat.

Hugh gave Boyd his attention once again. "And now Conall is the Earl of Bramton, but the union is not sanctioned by the king. Add to it Rory's marriage to Lady Freya. . . we are right and truly as much a target as you," he finished.

"You've been so for some time," Boyd said.

"Aye, but my parents have navigated their own ambitions with that of the king's."

"You think they will do so still?"

He shrugged. "There is to be a council meeting of the Northumbrian nobles. I sent Criseyde's men, and her maid, to Kenshire, where they will deliver the message that I am here, unable to attend. We shall see what they decide."

Boyd nodded. "Will you come with me to the training yard? Criseyde, you are welcome to join us if you'd like to see Hugh bested by his cousin."

"I thought Hugh the most confident man I'd met, more so than the king himself," she said, "but I'd not met Boyd Kerr, it seems."

"'Tis easy to be confident when you are assured of victory," Hugh said. "I will challenge Wallace instead. His sword arm is strong, but at least I've a chance at besting him."

"I would be pleased to join you." Criseyde said the words to Boyd, not him. Which was, he supposed, for the best.

CHAPTER 23
BOYD

Whatever the men in his family had been drinking, Boyd wanted no part of it.

As he'd done all day, Hugh watched Criseyde like a man who had never once eaten before. From the moment they sat for supper, at the same table as this morn, Hugh tried to avoid looking at her. When Boyd had questioned him earlier, he'd admitted to nothing.

"'Tis clear to anyone with eyes you are more than simply companions," he'd said, to which Hugh dismissed him.

"We will return tomorrow to Kenshire, where Criseyde will reunite with her men and return to France," was all the stubborn Waryn would say.

Even if Boyd did not have eyes, the evidence of Hugh's downfall could be heard in the clanging of swords that afternoon as they trained. He'd goaded Boyd into a sword-fight, which Boyd had won, of course. But to redeem himself with Criseyde watching, Hugh ensured it was the only challenge he would lose. By the end of the day, Wallace had begged him to remain, to aid in training the men that would come in the spring.

He denied Wallace, of course. While Hugh had fought with Clan Kerr many times, his place was in England. Or should be. Boyd's cousin did not wish to linger anywhere for long enough to know where he would remain.

For now, Boyd's place was here, but eventually it would be at Dunmure Tower where his parents lived. As the only son, he would inherit the holding where his father, Alex, had been raised. But Boyd did not wish to be lord over land ruled by the English bastard of a king. Thankfully, his cousin's companion had brought much-needed good tidings that could easily turn the tides of their fight.

As Hugh lifted his mug, Boyd began to laugh aloud.

"Share your good humor," Wallace said.

"I cannot. My cousin would not appreciate the direction of my thoughts." When he glanced first at the ale and then the woman next to him that Hugh had spent the day avoiding, his cousin's eyes narrowed.

"Then you would do well to keep those thoughts inside your head," Hugh said.

"You act more like brothers than cousins," Criseyde said.

"Indeed, I've spent more time at Kenshire, and both of us together at Bristol Manor, than we have apart. The Brotherhood convenes as many councils as they engage in battles."

"I so rarely hear the word spoken," Criseyde said.

"The Brotherhood?"

"Aye," she said.

"Some use it more than others, but all are grateful for the Waryn/Kerr alliance," Wallace said. But his voice held an ominous tone, and Boyd knew the reason well.

"William believes the time has come to declare," he said, saying what the outlaw was thinking. Wallace frowned.

"I do not disagree," Hugh said. "But you understand my family cannot openly declare for any king but their own."

"If Clan Kerr were to do so, the Waryns' support would be implied."

"You are allied with Robert the Bruce, are you not?" Criseyde asked Wallace.

He sighed as if the alliance were forced on him. "He is a better man than Balliol, and both than many of the other claimants."

"Clan Kerr does not agree?" she asked Boyd.

He thought on how to answer. "It is a complicated matter. In some ways it benefits our clan to ally with Wallace over any of the claimants to the throne."

"I," Wallace said with a wave of his hand, "am lord over this. A small holding in the woods and meager meal for my men. None covet what I've gained, and lost, since Stirling."

"But there will come a time your clan must openly declare," she said.

"'Tis astute of you to say as much, and I agree. Some would argue that time has come already, but our laird would not."

Criseyde looked at Hugh. "Is that Toren?"

He smiled as if she had achieved a great feat. Was Hugh done avoiding his lady then? He'd done so since the morn, and Boyd could not blame him. This was not a woman with whom he could trifle, but neither would his cousin marry.

Even if he was in love, a state Hugh had adamantly denied when questioned.

"It is. Boyd's father Reid and Toren, the chief, are brothers."

"There are as many Kerrs as there are Waryns, lass. But there is just one you should remember." Both he and Hugh waited for Wallace to finish. "Breac the Bold."

Boyd could not disagree. "Breac wields more influence than us all as Lord Warden of the Eastern Marches."

"Did you not say," Criseyde asked Hugh, "your father and brother both refused the position? On the English side of the border, of course."

"They did," Hugh agreed. "But their reasons for it, and why Breac will likely be the one Kerr to determine his clan's fate, is a story best told when we have more time."

"Or inclination to hear these two argue over politics," Wallace said. "Let there be no more talk of it this eve. Tonight, we celebrate."

All eyes turned to Criseyde. It was a brave thing she had done, traveling to these borders to pass on such a message. Although he did not wish for it himself, Boyd could understand his cousin's feelings for the woman.

Wallace led a toast, one of many that eve, until even Boyd had begun to dream of sleep. "I've an early watch," he said, standing. "I leave this night to you."

"Not I." Wallace stood as well. "Tomorrow I go for supplies."

Boyd frowned. "Would you not leave the task to someone else? To me?"

"Nay, I would not, and you know well I can remain here for so long."

"He takes risks," Boyd said, attempting to recruit Hugh in joining his bid to keep Wallace safe. "For the simple pleasure of a ride."

"Ride through the Ettrick Forest then," Hugh said, immediately taking up Boyd's cause. "If you are caught—"

"If I am caught, you will join your northern cousins to

wrest them free from that tyrant's grasp. Aye?" Without waiting for a response, he reached out a hand to Hugh, who stood. "God save you from harm on your journey home." He then turned to Criseyde, who stood as well. Bowing to her, he said, "My most fervent thanks to you, my lady. I will send men at the appointed time, and with your king's aid, we will defeat Edward come spring." Bowing, he continued, "I am forever in your debt."

She inclined her head. "I wish you well, and pray my king stands firm in his decision."

"If he does not, I will not blame you for the Frenchman's fickleness."

Criseyde smiled, not disagreeing with Wallace's assessment of King Philip.

"I bid you a good eve, and do hope you and Waryn make good use of my chamber."

Her jaw dropped, as did Hugh's, but Boyd was not a bit surprised. Though Wallace would never love another woman again by his own admission, the death of his wife having killed all hope of that, he was known to bed a lovely lass from time to time.

"As good a suggestion as you've ever had," Hugh whispered as Wallace walked away. Boyd did not think Criseyde heard him, but he had been watching his cousin and could see easily the words on his lips.

The two men exchanged a look, Boyd's a cautious one. But Hugh's look? Boyd could not quite tell.

CHAPTER 24

She'd wanted to speak to him, but Criseyde hadn't been certain of what to say precisely. Instead, she changed behind the screen and scrambled into bed. Was she being a coward?

Aye.

When they entered the chamber, Hugh looked as if he would ask her a question. Instead, he seemed to have changed his thinking. He laid down his sword and took off his belt before Criseyde decided he had naught to say to her.

Questions had swirled in her mind all day but one had nearly spilled from her lips earlier.

Why will you not look at me?

But the words never came. Besides, what else could she offer a man who so clearly did not wish for anything more than what they shared last eve? She'd told him she understood now, and she did. The women's whispers, their desire to take lovers...

Shamefully, she wanted it again.

Criseyde had forgotten herself in those moments.

Worries for her future, despair for the loss of the only man who'd truly loved her, a desire to keep the sense of independence she'd gained on this journey, all of them had disappeared. Like that first time when Hugh had taken her hand, claiming to be her husband, a feeling of warmth had overtaken her.

She didn't want to need a man, but Criseyde could easily find herself needing Hugh.

If she just said the words, rolled over now that Hugh was also in bed and uttered them—"I concede"—he would make love to her again. Criseyde was certain of it. Even though he'd avoided her the few times they'd exchanged a meaningful glance, his desire for her was still plain to see.

But Criseyde wanted more. She didn't want to want more, but wishing it away did little to banish the thought of returning to Kenshire with him and not returning to France. Which was, of course, absurd, as Hugh had made his derision for the idea of a wife clear.

The bed shifted.

Hugh's hand was suddenly on her hip. She could feel its warmth through the coverlet, but he did not move it. Nor would he, courtesy of their bet.

Say the words, Criseyde.

They would not come. She wanted him to touch her. To kiss her. To make love to her again. Wanted it so much Criseyde's chest felt heavy for the wanting. And still, the words did not come. She could not bring herself to submit to a man, even if that man were Hugh.

But neither could she bear the thought of Hugh removing his hand. And so she pulled down the coverlet so it now touched bare skin. At the silent invitation, he slid it upward, over her waist, until the very tips of his fingers brushed the side of her breast. They stayed there for a moment, and then his hand was on her. Cupping her. His thumb and forefinger rolled her nipple between them.

In response, Criseyde shifted closer to him, surprised to learn he wore nothing unlike the other times as Hugh pushed the coverlet completely down to the bottom of the bed with his feet. She moved in even closer, pressing her bottom to him, no longer frightened of the size of him even as she could feel every bit of Hugh against her buttocks.

As she pressed her hips into him, Hugh kissed the back of her shoulder. His hand left her breast as he used it to push her hair aside. Kissing her neck, and then just beneath her ear. . . he stopped.

Rolled her onto her back.

And then did something very curious. Hugh shifted himself toward the foot of the bed, which was when she realized what he was about. Criseyde had heard of men kissing women. . . there. But she'd certainly never experienced it with Etienne, nor would she have wished for such a thing.

Aye, she'd been right. Positioned between her legs, Hugh spread her wide. Pushing gently on her calves, he guided her to bend her knees while using his thumbs to open her.

And then kissed her.

Her hips jolted as his tongue began to move. It circled and teased her, and Criseyde was no longer silent now.

"Hugh, please," she begged for the second eve in a row. Now, however, Criseyde knew what she asked for. In response, he licked. Swirled. And even used his thumb as he'd done last eve. Criseyde's heart beat wildly, her legs beginning to shake.

When he stopped, Criseyde did not even have the chance to ask why before he was between her legs, now propped above her. With one swift motion, he was inside her. And Criseyde could not hold on. Not after what he'd done, with Hugh now filling her so completely. He thrust only twice before she called out his name. Three times and she began to quiver. That he watched her so intently made the spasms even stronger.

"Hugh," she said, the word hardly able to escape. Her voice did not even seem to be her own.

"Ahhh," Hugh breathed, his expression almost as if he were in pain. Pulling out from her, he leapt from the bed and grabbed a cloth from the table. She watched as he also found release, Criseyde wondering what it would be like for him to finish within her instead.

That she wanted that should have sent her screaming from the chamber. Instead, it made her sad to know she would never learn the answer to that question. Hugh may claim not to be a gentleman, but she knew the truth. He would not do it, not unless they were wed.

There is no woman alive who would wish for such a life.

His words were as clear in her mind as the day he'd said them. What would Hugh say to her if Criseyde told him she did not agree?

She wasn't certain she was prepared for his answer.

WHEN CRISEYDE WOKE, Hugh was gone. Since he'd refused to leave her alone in the keep, she assumed he was in the hall breaking his fast. Dressing with memories of the way his hand so tenderly moved up her body, and of course what he'd done to her, she wondered if Hugh would greet her as he'd done for most of their journey? Or would it be the Hugh that refused to even glance her way?

Unfortunately, as she entered the hall, it seemed the latter would be true. In fact, if possible, he was even more evasive today than the one before it. It was only when they'd prepared to leave, Criseyde and Hugh both mounted and ready to depart, that he spoke to her at any length at all.

"Boyd is in the woods, on guard," he said. "We will bid our farewell to him as we leave."

Hugh spurred his mount forward, and they began to ride. Hugh explained they would take the same route back east, passing just north of Bramton on their way to Kenshire. He grew silent once again until they came to the same bend in the road where Wallace had first emerged from the trees.

She neither heard nor saw Boyd until he was upon them.

"How are you so silent?" she asked as he rode toward them, seemingly having emerged from a thicket just along the road.

"When you train with the most hunted man on the isle, 'tis a necessary skill to learn."

Boyd rode to his cousin. "You will get a message to Bristol?"

"Aye. I will tell them that when Wallace finalizes a plan, you will send word."

"None can know of Philip's involvement yet."

"It would help to recruit men."

"It would," Boyd agreed. "But news of it would spread before the Frenchmen even reached our shores. We give them the number, though not the means, for now."

"It is agreed then. Until we meet again, cousin."

Boyd winked at her, and though she liked the man, Criseyde sensed he was very much like Hugh in many ways.

Both were the kind of men her friends at court always warned against. One such woman, Isabel of Dijon, knew well the pitfalls of thinking otherwise. All at court knew of her affair with a comte who had been known to discard the women who shared his bed. As she grew with child, the horrid man denied claims the babe was his and refused marriage. Criseyde knew well, as did all the ladies at court, that Isabel had been with no other man.

They'd traveled until the sun rose high above them before either she or Hugh spoke.

"We will stop here," he said, "to rest the horses."

She assumed he meant at the river's edge and so Criseyde navigated her mount toward it. This morn she'd thought to speak to him about last eve, and the one before. This silence between them was unnecessary. But Hugh had ridden ahead of her, even though they'd seen none on the road since Boyd. Not wishing to call out to him, she simply remained silent.

Criseyde had just dismounted when Hugh took her reins. She did not protest as he led them to the water. Never could she have imagined trading ball gowns for a leaf with which to wipe herself as she squatted, dress hiked to her thighs, behind a bush.

After handing her a piece of fresh bread, Hugh tied their mounts to a tree and stood at the river's edge looking at the water. Away from her.

"Where is the man who accompanied me here?" she asked, unable to tolerate his silence any longer. She stood beside him. "The one who shared my bed," Criseyde asked more quietly.

When Hugh did turn to her, his usual good humor was nowhere to be found. But neither had she expected the look he gave her. It was as if Hugh were in pain.

"Do you not realize," he said finally. "You must know two people do not come together usually in such a way."

"I do not understand."

Hugh looked back to the river that rushed past them. Criseyde did the same, watching as the rocks stood immovable no matter how fast the water greeted them.

"I wanted so badly to stay inside you. Never have I spilled my seed in any woman, but last eve. . ." He let out a breath. "I considered it, Criseyde. For longer than I should have."

"'Tis likely I cannot conceive a babe," she said.

"Or more likely your bastard of a husband could not."

"Hugh, look at me."

He did. "When I do, it's too easy to remember the feeling of you beneath me. Even now, I can almost taste you on my lips."

"You don't want to remember?" Criseyde's heart raced in a very different way than last eve, when Hugh's hand lay on her hip in a silent invitation.

"Nay," he said, his voice raised. "I do not."

Something simply broke apart inside her. Criseyde had endured much these past years, and on this journey, and she'd accept it all because she had no choice. But this, she would not accept.

"You are a coward, Hugh Waryn."

Hugh's lips pursed together, his eyes flashing.

"For a man so courageous, I do not understand how you admit defeat so easily now. You show me the greatest pleasure of my life but then turn from me as if I do not exist. I'd begun to think you were different from other men."

"I am no coward, Criseyde."

"With a sword"—she swung her hand wildly toward his horse—"or that damn axe you carry as a constant reminder to be stronger than your enemy. Nay, you are not. But to shun me because you dislike the feelings I arouse in you. What do you call that if not cowardly?"

He was listening, but Hugh apparently had no words to offer.

Criseyde spun from him, not willing to speak without being answered. Not willing to tell him what was in her heart if he could not hold her gaze.

She lifted her gown and stalked off, ignoring his call to her. When she stumbled on a loose rock, a pain shot through her ankle. She waved her arms out to steady her, but it was too late. To avoid her face hitting the ground, Criseyde leaned quickly to the left and tumbled directly into the river.

Her first thought when her head emerged above the water, aside from the cold, was that it could be so deep to submerge her. But then Criseyde had no opportunity to think of anything but keeping her head afloat. She tried to turn back, toward Hugh, but was not able.

Though she could swim courtesy of the small lake on her cousin's farm, it was not something one did for pleasure, and it had been many years since Criseyde found herself at Lago Sant'Erasmo.

It was futile to fight the current. Instead she attempted to swim to the bank, but even that proved difficult. Though she attempted to calm herself, it was becoming more and more difficult.

I do not want to die.

CHAPTER 25

The decision to jump in or run had taken only a moment. In the river, he could not see her. Instead, Hugh ran along the bank and called out to her as trees flew by him. When she'd begun to stumble, he'd only wanted to save her from a fall.

Now, Hugh attempted to save her life.

Each time he'd thought of the real possibility that Criseyde could not keep her head above the river's waters, that she could be swept away from him in front of his very eyes, he could hardly keep from losing his stomach. This could not possibly be happening.

Except, it was.

Criseyde's head bobbed up and down as he ran, Hugh very quickly losing the training he'd so finely honed. Keeping control of his thoughts, not allowing panic to overcome him, could cost a man his life in battle. And was not something he'd struggled with before. Until now.

Thankfully his body did not hesitate where his mind failed him. He searched for a spot to jump into the river without losing her. He yelled to her, told her to swim closer to the bank. But she did not hear him.

She will not die. I love you, Criseyde. I love you, and you will not die today.

She'd called him a coward, and his anger had not been toward her but himself. Why had he been spared that day? Hugh still did not fully know his place as a Waryn. He knew only his desire to protect those he loved mattered above all, and Criseyde counted among them.

"Criseyde," he called, aware his voice was now frantic but unable to stop himself. "Criseyde, swim toward me," he screamed, even knowing she could not hear him.

Twice he stumbled along the rocky bank, and twice he kept his footing. He'd hoped for a bend, for some respite from the slight downhill terrain that gave the river's water its powers. And then, he lost her. Having turned for the briefest of moments to ensure his own footing, he lost her.

"Criseyde," he called again, wanting to jump so badly into those waters but knowing he could not do so blindly. He'd never find her."

No. No, no, no.

The river began to widen, the strength of its waters abating just slightly. He saw her then and did not hesitate. Hugh was just enough ahead of her that he would not be forced to fight the current to reach her. He jumped in, the cold of the water taking away his breath. Another fear he'd had, but Hugh could not think on that now. He swam to her, Criseyde's arm nearly eluding him as he reached out to grasp it. He would not let her go.

Not now. Not ever.

He had her, but Criseyde did not respond to him. He had to get her out of this river. Though her strength had long since left her, Hugh's had not. He swam them to the bank and pulled Criseyde from the water. She was shivering, but alive. Crying, but Hugh cared for only one thing now. Getting her warm. He stripped off her gown and lifted her into his arms, holding her to his chest. Her eyes were closed, but she breathed. The blessed rise and fall of her chest was so sweet that tears sprang to his eyes even as he spied the blood on her side. She'd cut herself, on a rock most likely. He would check it, but Hugh did not think the cut was deep.

He could not stop there. He walked as fast as possible back toward the horses, knowing she needed warmth. The saltiness of his tears seeped onto his lips, its taste one he had never known. Without risking dropping her, he moved more quickly, amazed at how far they had come in such a short time.

Finally reaching their mounts, he worked quickly. Laying her on the ground, he pulled up her shift to assure himself the cut was indeed a small one. Satisfied, he covered Criseyde with the one blanket he carried, then gathered firewood. It took much longer than he'd hoped, finding dry wood a challenge, but finally, after what seemed like an eternity, he had a fire lit, though they were closer to the road than he would like.

Stripping his own wet clothes off and laying them on the ground, he carried Criseyde to the fire, removed her boots and shift, and held her to him. He welcomed her shivers. She was alive, and would remain so. Hugh would not let death have her today.

Criseyde di Vilardino was his. And when she woke, he would tell her so.

~

HUGH WASN'T certain how long he held her in his arms, but oddly, he was not afraid. She *would* open her eyes. He sat with his back to a tree trunk, Criseyde curled against him and covered with a red and green plaid that his cousin Galien had once given him.

For so long he'd questioned his purpose, his position in his family. The reason he was left alive during that attack. Now such a sentiment felt foolish. She was right. Perhaps Criseyde was that purpose. Or if not, they would discover it together.

Finally, as he watched her eyelids flutter, Criseyde looked at him.

She said nothing for some time, as if she were uncertain how she found herself nude, though no longer wet, in his arms.

"I'm not cold," she said, a question in her voice.

"I am glad to hear it." Leaning his head down, Hugh kissed her. It was the softest of kisses they'd shared. His lips glided over hers, Hugh's tongue only touching Criseyde's when hers tentatively sought his. The kiss quickly became something it should not after what she'd endured. Reluctantly, he pulled away.

"You saved my life."

"Nay, Criseyde, you saved mine."

Her brows furrowed. Though she did not yet understand, she would. But now that she was awake, they needed to move.

"We've much to discuss. But we will not reach Kenston House tonight, and I've no provisions for us to sleep under the stars."

"What will we do?" Criseyde asked, shivering as he removed the plaid.

"I've an idea, but we must be on our way."

He realized something was amiss as soon as he stood and attempted to make Criseyde stand with him.

"My ankle," she said, shifting her weight. "I twisted it when I fell."

Hugh immediately set her down and went to the saddlebag. He pulled out Criseyde's remaining gown and helped to dress her.

"You are not quite as adept as Elizabeth," she teased.

"I am more accustomed to removing gowns," he said. When he finished, Hugh took clothing from his saddlebag and dressed himself, sensing her eyes on him. "Keep looking at me that way and we will certainly be sleeping here," he said, indicating the small fire.

"How?" she asked, also looking at the fire. "Is not the wood all wet?"

Dressed, he reached down and scooped her up in his arms.

"Where is my riding gown?"

Hugh nodded toward the river. "Discarded where I pulled you onto the bank."

As they walked, she continued to ask questions.

"How did you pull me from that river?"

He thought of the moment he'd lost her, not wishing to relive it. "I ran alongside the bank until I could get in front of you. You are safe, Criseyde," he said as she shivered.

"I am safe," she said, as if convincing herself.

A lump formed in his throat. He would say more, but Hugh could not. The memory of her in that water was too fresh. Too disturbing to relive just now. He lifted her onto his mount and untied both horses. It was only when he seated himself behind her, Criseyde's mount riding along-side them as he clutched her reins as well as his own, that he said softly, "I was more scared this day than any of my life. We must talk, Criseyde. I cannot lose you."

She turned in the saddle, her hair wet, her eyes still filled with wildfire despite her ordeal, and said, "Thank you for saving me."

Again, tears threatened, so he did not answer. He wanted to do more than simply say the words. Instead, he kissed her once again before spurring his mount forward. They still had a long journey ahead.

CHAPTER 26

"What is this place?"

She'd fallen asleep in Hugh's arms and woke cold and shivering again. Despite it, she sat up in the saddle, curious. Criseyde had never seen such buildings as the ones before her. They looked like farmhouses made of stone.

"I think it best for you to see for yourself."

No sooner had the words left his lips than the last man she'd have expected to stride toward them did so with a grin.

"You were expecting us," Hugh said to the reiver.

"Of course."

"She's injured, Ulric," he said, and the man's grin fled. The same one who'd attempted to rob her now held his arm up as if to help her. "She cannot stand on her left foot and her side needs tending."

"Come now," he said, the overly large man lifting her down as easily as Hugh had carried her by the river. "I will not harm you."

The moment Hugh dismounted, he scooped her up into his arms again.

"I can walk," she argued, but he ignored her.

"She needs a fire for warmth and fresh bandages," Hugh said as Ulric motioned for a boy to take their horse and began to lead her and Hugh to one of the strange manor houses. It was a small makeshift village of sorts.

"Were you attacked?" Ulric asked as they walked toward the largest of the stone structures.

"Nay. Criseyde stumbled into the river."

"And nearly drowned," she added. "Hugh saved my life at great risk to his own."

"I am unsurprised to hear it," was all Ulric said. Indeed, it seemed as if Hugh told her the sun would rise in the morn and not that he'd jumped into a river to save her. Did he do such things often?

"I can walk," she said as Hugh began to climb the wooden stairs. They were the only thing in sight made of wood.

"In an attack," he said, "these can be burned."

"Could not an attacker bring a ladder?"

Ulric chuckled in front of them.

"Aye," Hugh answered. "But the type of men these bastle houses defend against are not ones who bring ladders."

They'd reached the top. Ulric opened the door, and all three of them stepped into a living space. It was like a second-floor hall, though its ceiling was not as high. Partway into the hall, another ladder led to a loft, which appeared to be a sleeping space.

"My family is abed," Ulric said, indicating the loft. "Sit by the fire," he added as he walked toward the ladder.

They sat on seats of stone with cushions placed on

them, the fire in the center of the room. She looked up to see the smoke escaping through a roof vent.

"Give your feet to me," Hugh said, sitting beside her. When she did so, he removed her wet boots. He held her feet toward the fire, warming them also with his hands. Hugh said nothing, but the way he looked at her...

We've much to discuss.

Criseyde was uncertain what Hugh had meant, but from his expression now, she could venture a guess. Something had shifted between them, and Criseyde could no longer deny that she had fallen in love with Hugh Waryn. She'd fallen in love with a man that did not wish for a wife, and certainly Criseyde had not come to England to find a husband. And yet, the thought of returning to France, which had not felt like home since her father left her, never seeing Hugh again...

"You are still cold?"

"Nay," she said as Ulric returned.

"I've dried fruit and bread," he said, putting a wooden tray beside them. "My wife sleeps so I did not wake her. In the morn, we will supply you with all you need for your journey."

"We thank you for your hospitality."

"It is given gladly to the son of Geoffrey Waryn. A bed is being prepared below in the stable loft. My apologies," he said to Criseyde.

"None are needed," she said. "I care not where I lay my head. A stable loft is most preferred over a watery grave."

Hugh winced. It seemed he did not care for the reminder.

"My apologies are for attempting to rob you."

"You would do so again if she were not with me," Hugh

teased, her feet still in his hands. He rubbed them, pressing with his thumbs, but stopped when he spoke.

Criseyde wiggled her toes, and he began to rub again. No one had ever done such a thing to her, and she quite enjoyed it, though perhaps not as much as other things he did to her.

"I would," Ulric admitted. "I leave you to the fire," he said then, adding a log to it.

He disappeared again up the ladder.

"You wish me to continue?" Hugh asked.

The fire crackled as Criseyde shifted on her cushion. She nodded. "I would not have expected to be here that day we came upon Ulric and his men."

"I would not have expected to confess my love to you the day I spied you in my cousin's hall." He said it so casually Criseyde was uncertain if she'd heard him correctly. "I thought I'd lost you, Criseyde. When I did not, I realized finally, after so many years, why I'd been spared that day of the attack."

He did stop rubbing then, but Criseyde did not wiggle her feet. Instead she stared at him, waiting for his next words.

"It was so that I might find you."

Her cheeks tingled with unshed tears. "Hugh," was all she managed to say.

"I will not let you go, Criseyde."

She said the words back to him that had been etched into her memory since the day he uttered them. "There is no one woman alive who could sate me," Criseyde repeated.

He shook his head, pushed her feet from his lap, and moved to her, putting his arm around her shoulder. "I was a fool to think it, and more of one to say the words. I love you,

Criseyde. I will remain at Kenshire, find a purpose there if you will agree to be my wife."

His free hand moved to her cheek. Criseyde covered it with one of her own, her eyes never leaving his. "I'd not remain at Kenshire with you." The hurt in his eyes at her words told Criseyde all she needed to know of his true feelings. She continued, "For you are not a man content to remain in one place."

"I will do so, for you."

"There is no need," she explained, assuring him. "I would go where you go. I remained at court for many years and have no need for such entrapments. Being on the road these past days with you has been more of an adventure than I ever could of hoped for and one I dearly wish to continue. What I do need though is you, even if it gives me some discomfort to say it."

"Criseyde." He kissed her so tenderly Criseyde could feel his love for her. "You could do anything you wished to do without me. You came here, delivered your message. . . I've not met a woman braver than you. But let me protect you. Let me love you."

She did not hesitate. "If you accept my love, then I will gladly accept yours."

This time when he kissed her, Criseyde did not hold back. She forgot about the rub, about the burden of her message, and even about that terrifying moment she realized in the river she could no longer hold on.

All that mattered now was this kiss.

This man.

CHAPTER 27

"Your axe? 'Tis gone?"

The morning they'd left the reivers, Criseyde still riding with him and unable to fully stand on her ankle, he'd looked first at her and then at Ronan's axe, which hung from the saddle. He'd said it was a reminder not to be taken unaware, to be stronger than his enemy. Instead it had reminded him that he had lived when some of his friends had not. Each time he looked at it, Hugh wondered why he had been spared, what purpose he served.

But it was not the reminder of that day that made Hugh strong. It was something he'd fought against. Chided his brother and cousin for feeling. Love had him battle that river's current more fiercely than he'd fought in any battle. And it was love for his family that took him from east to west and across the border into Scotland.

He needed no other purpose. Nor did he need a reminder of it.

"It had been gone for days," he said, Criseyde's backside wiggling into him nearly making Hugh forget her injury.

Sleeping beside her each night, not wishing to harm her any further as Criseyde's waist healed, was the worst torture he'd ever endured, save those horrific moments in the river.

"Where is it?"

"Tossed in a stream, no longer needed."

He could not see her face, but Criseyde asked no other questions. That he did not have to explain the axe's absence because she understood was one of the many reasons he loved her. And perhaps had from the moment he discovered her leaving Sutwork before dawn after having been beset by Ulric's men the day before. It was Criseyde who'd ordered them to leave. The woman knew no fear.

It was some time later, as Hugh had just been contemplating moving Criseyde's hair to the side and kissing her on the neck, that she squealed his name. Looking up, he saw what she did below the ridge they'd climbed earlier. From this vantage point, his home was as spectacular a sight as any Hugh had ever seen.

Kenshire Castle.

Built on top of a high basalt crag overlooking expansive sands and the wild North Sea, it was the largest castle in all of Northumbria. His grandfather had been responsible for many of Kenshire's additions, and the comforts Criseyde would find inside were courtesy of his parents' ability to thus far avoid Edward's many attempts at reclaiming some of the earldom's power.

"It is as spectacular as any castle I've seen," she said, turning back to him. Hugh had no need to look at a home he knew well. Instead, he stared into the eyes of the woman that would become his wife. He would speak to his parents and the priest the moment they arrived. Hugh had no wish to sleep separated from her, but he knew already his mother would insist on it until they were married.

"Not more spectacular than you. Are you certain you wish to remain here? You will not miss Paris?"

"My answer is the same as it's been each time you asked. There is nothing for me at that court. Even France, though it was my home for many years, was not somewhere that felt like home, especially after my father passed away. But you know this already."

"I do," he said. "But I would be certain. These are tumultuous times here along the border."

"Are they?" she asked, spinning even more toward him. "I did not realize as much when the king tasked me with bringing that message to Wallace. But now I understand why I was made to learn all the names of those sympathetic to the outlaw's cause. 'Tis dangerous." She said the word in a conspiratorial whisper.

He kissed her nose. "Your jest is not amusing," he said, ruining his words by grinning widely.

"Is it not?"

"Nay, it is not."

"Hmm, 'tis a shame that my side feels as if it is mostly healed. If you do not find me amusing, then you will not wish to share my bed this eve."

"I have altered my thinking," he said immediately. "Though I fear I must sneak into your chamber if my mother has her way."

Criseyde immediately turned serious. "I would not do so and have your mother think ill of me."

"She would not do so," he said, realizing for the first time. "You are so similar in many ways. 'Tis remarkable, in fact."

"Tell me," she said, leaning backward into him.

Hugh began riding once again, and as they headed toward Kenshire, he gladly told Criseyde of his mother. "When her father died, her cousin, Sir Randolf, claimed the title of earl of Kenshire despite my mother's own stronger claim. My grandfather, Richard Caiser, anticipated as much and protected against it by soliciting his friends to protect her."

"His friends? You mean, the reivers?"

"Aye, men who many might call dishonorable."

"But not you?"

They rode closer and closer to Kenshire Castle. "I ask myself, what is honor? If 'tis to regard others with respect, my father's friends are the most honorable men I know."

"But not to those who cross their path and find their belongings taken from them?"

"Nay," he agreed. "Not to them. But if you take from a man who is known for excess, who himself does not honor others, what is it then? How do you define the actions of both?"

"Some would say 'tis not for us to define. That can be left only to God."

"And you," he asked. "What would you say?"

"I would say that you called yourself dishonorable when you are anything but that. 'Tis difficult, I think, to name it either yea or nay. The word matters less than a man or woman's actions."

"I agree," he said as they followed the slope down to the outer wall of Kenshire. "And am pleased for you to say as much."

"Why?" she asked, though Criseyde did not press the matter.

"Because I would like to act honorably this eve when my mother insists on separate chambers, as I know she will, but I'd also like to visit you this eve." He leaned closer, whispering into her ear. "And if your side is truly healed, I would make love to you as we've done, but this eve, I'd not pull from you. Instead, I would happily come inside you, after I've made you moan in pleasure more than once, of course."

If he'd hoped to have Criseyde anticipate their evening together, Hugh had failed miserably. Instead, he could not sit on his mount correctly, and would likely be unable to dismount easily unless he thought of something besides Criseyde.

"'Tis magnificent," she said in response, looking toward the castle gates before them.

"Aye," he agreed until Criseyde turned back to him, and then looked down between them as if speaking of his manhood. The minx was taunting him, attempting to get a rise from him with her words, and she was doing spectacularly. Thankfully they had road ahead of them on which to travel.

"Is your side truly healed?"

"I believe it is," Criseyde said.

"Good," he said, turning her words against her. "I will show you magnificent this eve, putting to rest any thoughts you had before today of the meaning of the word."

CHAPTER 28

Criseyde had been to King Philip's apartments many times with her father. She'd met some of the most important nobles from many countries and had accepted a mission that she'd known would be quite dangerous. But never had Criseyde been as worried as this moment.

Likely the earl and countess of Kenshire had thoughts on their son's marriage that did not include wedding a nearly impoverished widow from France. Though Hugh had attempted to reassure her otherwise, Criseyde was wise to the ways of the nobility, and by all accounts, the Waryns were the most important family in Northumbria. Their eldest son had married well, though not of their choosing, as Hugh's brother had married for love.

"I've not seen you like this," Hugh said beside her as they moved from the stables toward the main keep. It had just grown dark, but Kenshire Castle was still visible courtesy of torches everywhere. There was no doubt any foe approaching this place would be intimidated to attack. According to Hugh, none had attempted it since his mother's cousin tried to claim Kenshire from his mother many years ago. Now Criseyde could see the reason for it.

"Ours is a hasty union," she said. "If King Philip offers my reward—"

"He had best not consider holding it or we will be battling two kings."

She smiled. "You would go to war with France for a bit of coin?"

"I would go to war with France to defend your honor. And we would win too."

When they'd first met, Criseyde would have taken his words as arrogance, but now she knew better than that. He truly believed them, and she could not be certain the Waryns, with their many powerful alliances, could best Philip himself.

Criseyde would have responded, but the moment the doors of the keep were opened, a young woman came running toward them. For a moment, her heart sank seeing the pure joy on the woman's face. But reason quickly intervened and she realized it was his sister.

"You've been away so long," she said, letting him go and then looking straight at Criseyde. Hugh had described his sister as brazen, a "hoyden through and through." Criseyde had chided him at the time for the description, but now understood it. The queen of France was not as confident as this woman.

"Haddie, I am pleased to introduce you to—"

"Lady Criseyde. The Italian-born French woman who defied you." Her face lit up with a smile. "I adore you already. Hugh thinks much too highly of himself."

For that, Hugh swatted her arm.

"My son."

Before she had an opportunity to respond, the most

beautiful dark-haired woman, one who looked precisely like her daughter but older, as Hugh had described, strode toward them. The servants had all moved away to afford them this reunion.

If she'd not already been in love with Hugh, Criseyde would have fallen for him when she saw his expression just then. It was pure joy and love all combined into one, and tears immediately formed in Criseyde's eyes. She knew the feeling. It was how she'd felt about her father, as if all was well in the world when he was there.

As they embraced, Lady Sara's hand moved toward Hugh's and held it even after they moved apart. It was odd to her, to see a man so formidable as Hugh holding his mother's hand, but the sight was endearing too.

"My mother worries when I go," Hugh said to Criseyde. "Where we went."

"And you must be Lady Criseyde?"

"I am," Criseyde said, bowing to the countess. "And pleased to make your acquaintance."

"As am I. The meal is underway," she said, and then to Hugh, "We'd heard you passed through the gates and have places set for you if you'd like to eat."

Criseyde looked down to her gown. "I could not grace your hall in this," she said. "It has been the only gown I've worn since. . ." She did not wish to burden Lady Sara now with the story.

"Since Criseyde stumbled into a river and nearly drowned," Hugh said for her, moving to Criseyde's side. "Which is when I realized how much I loved her and would not be parted from her if she would have me."

Hugh held her hand now. Criseyde hadn't been expecting that announcement to come so quickly, and her heart began to pound as the words tumbled from his lips.

Criseyde was not certain whether Lady Sara or her daughter were more surprised. She could not bear to see their reaction. Instead she turned to Hugh, looking up at him, unsure what to say. He smiled reassuringly before Criseyde turned her attention back to the women.

Lady Sara seemed pleased enough, but it was Haddie who surprised her. Grabbing her hand, she pulled on her arm. "Come with us," she said. "We will finish our meal in my mother's chambers. Hugh, eat quickly and join Father in the village. There has been a fire."

"A fire?" Hugh seemed rightly alarmed.

"The blacksmith's shop," Sara explained. "It is contained apparently."

"And must be out already," he said. "For we saw no flames on the way here."

"Good. But perhaps Haddie is right. I am pleased, son," she said. "We welcome Criseyde to our family and will take care of her this eve."

"I would not leave her," he said, but Haddie waved her hand as if impatient.

"Go to Father. We will love her more than you," she said. "Eat quickly and be gone. I wish to hear all of Criseyde's tale.

Hugh smiled. "So she is Criseyde already then?"

It was not common to drop one's title without being given permission, yet Haddie did not seem the kind of woman who cared much for conventions other than her own.

Criseyde liked her immensely already.

"She will be your wife, so aye."

"We will take care of her," Lady Sara said.

Criseyde nodded. "Go to your father."

"Her ankle is tender," he said, though Criseyde waved him off.

"I am fine. Go to your father."

Hugh issued a silent apology to her, but none was needed. With a final glance at all three women, he walked quickly toward what she assumed was the great hall. Tugging on her hand, Haddie led her in the opposite direction.

"If Haydn was surprised, Hugh is even more so. Of course, Blase will not marry for some time, and if I have my way, I will not do so until I love a man as well, which is unlikely to happen here at Kenshire as I am."

"Perhaps we should let Criseyde speak," Lady Sara said as they moved toward a set of stairs. "Would you like assistance?" she asked.

Though it pained her slightly when she stood on it fully, Criseyde shook her head. "It is mending." At the top of the stairs, they turned to the right, and Criseyde was well lost already. Lady Sara unlocked one of two double doors in front of them and pushed it open. Her solar chamber was beautiful, decorated with so many colors and bright tapestries that it felt as if Criseyde could be back at court. And yet, there was a warmth to her rooms too.

"Come and sit with us. Food and drink are being brought and your own chambers readied. When we are finished, a bath will be waiting already," Lady Sara said.

Criseyde had not even seen her speak to a servant, yet her efficiency was unsurprising. This was a woman to be admired, and Criseyde had expected no less. Sure enough, before they'd even settled themselves, wooden trays of food and wine followed them. It was only after all three women sat at a table large enough to host five others that Hugh's mother asked about their journey.

"Hugh and I did not care much for each other," she admitted, to Haddie's laugh.

"I do not care for him often," she said, ignoring the stern look from her mother. "He is nearly as arrogant as Blase," she argued even as Lady Sara looked at her as if she wished Lady Haddie would stop talking. "I am sorry, Mother, but 'tis true. They are like their father in many ways."

Finally, Lady Sara's lips turned up just slightly. "I suppose this is true." And then to Criseyde, "I must admit, I did not take kindly to Hugh's father, a reiver, coming here to Kenshire with his uncle to protect me." She said the word "protect" as if it were a curse.

"Hugh told me all of what transpired. He speaks so fondly of your capabilities, my lady."

"Sara," the countess said, for which Criseyde was grateful. "May I call you Criseyde?"

"Of course," she said immediately. "I would be grateful if you both did so, as I am grateful for your kind reception."

"Tell us how you fell in love with my brother."

"Haddie," Sara chastised her.

"I am curious, Mother. Are you not as well?"

Between bites of the most delicious fish she'd ever eaten, Criseyde attempted to explain. "When we learned we both supported the same cause, Hugh insisted on traveling to Wallace's camp without my companions. I've not had the opportunity to ask of their wellbeing?"

"Your maid, Elizabeth, has fallen for the marshal's son," Haddie said. "She will be pleased to learn you are staying at Kenshire."

"Haddie," Lady Sara scolded.

"Your men are well, as is your maid. They told us of your run-in with Ulric and his men."

"Allora," she said, realizing belatedly she'd switched to Italian. Criseyde used it rarely but found the language of her birthplace finding its way into her speech from time to time. "After I fell into the river—a tale I've no wish to relive except that it brought Hugh and I together—we stayed with Ulric and his family for one eve."

"He is a good friend of my husband's," Sara said. Criseyde attempted not to stare at the woman. She was so lovely and poised. "I believe it is Hugh's way to connect with his father in a way neither Haydn nor Holt have done. His friendship with the reivers—"

"Friendship? Mother, he raids with them."

Sara did not address Haddie's claim, which Criseyde knew to be true. "I am glad you are safe," was all she said.

Criseyde made certain Sara understood. "I am safe only because your son dove into the river that had nearly overtaken me to save my life."

"I'd not have wished you to experience such a trial."

"In a way," she said quietly, Criseyde and Hugh having discussed the matter, "it has hastened our attachment to each other. I'd fallen in love with your son—your brother—but he was not prepared to marry."

"Until he nearly lost you," Haddie said, surprisingly quiet.

"Aye," she said.

"You will not miss France?" Haddie asked.

"Nay." The question was an easy enough one to answer. "My mother died in childbirth. My father, who moved us from Italy to France, passed a few years ago along with my husband in the sweating sickness."

"I am so sorry," Sara said, her eyes genuinely sad for her. "I too lost a father when I was but your age. But you have a family now, Criseyde, and we are pleased to welcome you to it."

Criseyde had no words. So instead she thanked her and finished eating, wondering when she would see Hugh again. As if on cue, Haddie asked her about a wedding and she and Lady Sara began to discuss the preparations that must be made as if it was done. As if there was nothing more to discuss.

Hugh had come home with her on his arm, announced he was in love and wished to be with Criseyde, and his family took the news more easily than a countess should have done. By the time the meal was ended, Criseyde understood Hugh better and could see easily where he got his good nature from.

But there was one person yet to meet, and from Hugh's description, it was his father that Hugh's fearsome side was from. She would not count her blessings just yet. Not until she met Geoffrey Waryn, earl of Kenshire.

And it seemed she might do so sooner than she was ready for as the heavy wooden door swung open.

CHAPTER 29

Hugh was exhausted for not having slept all eve. Despite it, he wished only to see Criseyde, yet none knew where she slept. He'd asked the servants, and not one person seemed to know which chamber his mother had installed her in—an oddity, since they typically knew everything. But the fire that had nearly been put out when he and Criseyde made their way to the castle had flared up again with a vengeance. He worked alongside his father and the other men to save the blacksmith's shop and nearby buildings, but unfortunately it had not been spared.

"Get some rest, son. You will see her in the morn."

Hugh looked up to the sky, unsure how his father knew what he'd been thinking, as the two made their way across the courtyard. "'Tis nearly morn now," he said. "I am sorry we were not able to save it."

Geoffrey Waryn, a man more intimidating than any other alive with a wildness not typical of most earls, laid his hand on Hugh's arm so gently none would believe it if they spied the two men. From him, Hugh had learned that kindness was not weakness, that even the most fearsome of warriors could show affection. He had never been grateful for the lesson before now.

"You did well. The shop can be rebuilt and much was saved for our efforts."

His father had not yet removed his hand. Though their reunion had been brief, Hugh had told his father what Criseyde's companions had not: that he wished to marry her. It seemed their discussion about the subject, one Hugh had thought would wait until they'd slept, would come now.

"You are in love with her?"

Hugh had never been as certain of anything as he was his answer to this question.

"Aye."

"Then we shall have a wedding. A cause for celebration is much needed." His hand dropped and the men began walking once again.

"The alliances you oft spoke of—"

His father cut him off. "Mean less to me than your happiness, Hugh. Though her father is a right bastard, your brother's union with Phillipa has brought all Kenshire a union that strengthens it. That Haydn found love as well is a boon none expected."

"I will make you proud, Father," he said quietly. "You will love Criseyde as I do."

"I've no doubt of it. And you already make me proud, Son."

His chest swelled, Hugh never tiring of the words but, for the first time, he actually believed him. "I will fight for our cousin's cause," he said, resolved. "If Criseyde could risk everything to deliver a message to Wallace, I would do so as well."

More than his union with Criseyde, it was that bit of news he worried most to tell his father. But Hugh was resolved.

His father sighed. "I've yet to tell you of the council meeting."

Hugh knew that tone. "Did it not go well?"

"Nay, it did not." They'd reached the keep. All was quiet still, the sun not yet risen. Hugh waited for his father to say more, but instead he gestured for Hugh to climb the steps in front of them. "Sleep. We will talk more later." When he smiled, the wrinkles at the corner of his eyes and bits of gray hair sprinkled throughout his head did not diminish that his father was still very much a good-looking man. "I am looking forward to meeting the woman that brought you to your knees."

Hugh may not have put it in such a way, but he could not argue with his father's assessment. For a moment, he thought of her in that river, and then of Criseyde's own father. The thought that there would be a day Hugh would come home and his father would not be here to greet him. . . it was something he thought little of, but as he did so now, Hugh wrapped his arms around him. He could not think of a time in recent memory when he'd done so, hugged his father in anything other than a quick greeting. But now, being held in his arms as if he were a boy, he was sorry he'd not done it more often.

"No man had a father better than you."

In response, his father held him tighter and even grabbed Hugh's tunic at his back. He said nothing, as was his way, but the gesture was enough. More than enough, in fact.

It was precisely what Hugh needed.

HE'D NEVER DRESSED SO QUICKLY in his life.

Hugh had fallen asleep after he and his father returned, his bed at Kenshire usually a welcome respite. But not this time. He'd become accustomed to having Criseyde next to him. Fairly running into the hall, he greeted members of the household less warmly than he might otherwise. Hugh just wanted to see her.

He paused at the entrance.

The morning meal was well underway, and though the hall was filled with more than twenty retainers, there was just one person he wished to see.

Criseyde's transformation wasn't something he expected. If the bedraggled woman he'd pulled from the river was beautiful, the lady before him was simply spectacular. She sat at the head table, next to Haddie. Thus far, Criseyde hadn't noticed him. She and Hugh's sister spoke, amicably it seemed, though he was unsurprised. The two women were more similar than different, though it was Criseyde alone he stared at now. She wore a deep purple velvet gown inlaid with gold thread. Its sleeves hung low, but Criseyde lifted her goblet, navigating them easily. She belonged here. It had been easy on the road for him to forget she was a woman of the court.

When she looked across the hall, their eyes met. Hugh remembered, finally, to walk again and he made his way to the table. Before taking his place beside his father, Hugh greeted the women. But mostly, he greeted Criseyde.

"Good morn," he said to her, and then to his mother. "I trust you slept well?"

"Indeed," she said, the smile in her voice confirming what Hugh had already suspected. He addressed Criseyde. "You slept in the lord and lady's tower last eve?"

"I did."

"Thank you, Mother, for keeping such a close watch on Criseyde." He cleared his throat. "I meant to say, for taking such good care of her."

His father laughed aloud, but Hugh ignored him. "Haddie," he said by way of a greeting before climbing the stairs to the dais. Once seated, he attempted to eat but found it difficult. He simply wanted her alone. He wanted to kiss her, to make love to her. To talk of their wedding and their future. Instead, he was forced to endure the longest meal in recent memory.

"Tell me of the council," he asked his father, unable to speak easily to Criseyde with three people between them. He would have to remember to thank his mother later for placing her at the head table. Normally she'd not do so until they were wed, and surely Criseyde understood its significance. She was already well and truly welcomed into the family.

"It did not go well. We can agree on nothing except a mutual dislike for Edward's tactics."

"Haydn and Holt have left already?"

"Aye. Haydn and Phillipa back to Hillstone Manor and Holt to rejoin his cousin for a tourney in Barrington."

"Who else attended?"

"Helmsley, Brookhurst, deCrecy, Lyndwood—"

"That crusty old bastard made the journey?"

"He did."

As his father told him of all the Northumbrian lords who traveled to Kenshire, he tried to hide his alarm as

Criseyde often peeked over at him. To her, he offered only smiles. But to his father, just the opposite.

"If we are not united, Edward will take advantage. He will continue to demand men to fight his blasted battles, and there will be more tragedies like Bramton."

His father did not disagree. "Even so, 'tis not the time to fight openly with your cousins against him. Edward is our king, and if I'd avoid Bramton's fate, you'd do well to remember it."

When his father used that tone, Hugh knew better than to disagree. "You said 'openly.'"

The earl frowned. "We can no longer ignore the fact that sides will need to be chosen."

"They have already," he reminded him.

His father sighed. "Aye, they have." Likely noticing Hugh looking at Criseyde, he added, "But first, we've a wedding to plan."

Somehow Haddie heard his father's words. "The planning is well underway."

He and Criseyde exchanged a look. No longer hungry, at least for food, he could wait no longer. "I would give you a tour of Kenshire," he said to Criseyde, ignoring the sound Haddie made in her throat. "If that pleases you?"

"It would please me very much," she said, her eyes darting to the countess.

"Mother," he said, fixing that particular problem. "Do you not have much to do if we're to have a wedding at Kenshire?"

Thankfully, she took the hint. "Indeed." Standing, indicating the meal had in fact ended, she said to Criseyde, "I would not presume to plan for you—"

"There is but one detail that concerns me, and that is

the presence of your son. All else, I defer to your clearly capable hands."

If his mother seemed pleased, Haddie was even more so.

But none were more pleased than him. Hugh knew precisely where he would take Criseyde.

CHAPTER 30

After spending so much time with Hugh these past days, she should not feel shy with him now. But as they left the hall, Criseyde found herself stealing glances at him as if they'd not spent most nights sharing the same bed, as if they'd not made love already.

So much had happened, and so quickly, that when she had shared her news with Elizabeth, she expected the maid to be shocked. Instead, she had simply smiled and said she was not surprised. That Sir Hugh was "a man worthy of your attention, and no more so than you are of his." But that was not the best news of all.

"Elizabeth wishes to stay," she said, following Hugh from the keep to Kenshire's stables.

"I'm glad to hear it." He looked at Criseyde the same way he had before their first kiss. As then, her heart sped up at the prospect. "I'm sorry for having left you last eve. When we returned it was nearly sunrise and none seemed to know where you stayed."

Criseyde smiled. "Your mother may have mentioned

184

hiding me away from you until the wedding. She knows you well."

"Aye," he agreed. "She does. I'd have come to you no matter the hour."

"And I'd have welcomed you."

Before he could respond, a man emerged from the stables. He was bearded, his hair long but tied behind him. "We meet again," he said, looking toward Criseyde.

"It has been too long." Hugh laughed and explained to her. "Sir Reginald is Kenshire's marshal. Reginald, I am pleased to introduce my betrothed, Lady Criseyde."

Betrothed. Though not quite true as no papers had been signed, Criseyde liked the sound of it. "Word has spread quickly, my lady, so I cannot profess surprise at your presence. Though I'm pleased to meet the woman who's brought Hugh to his heels."

"As I am," she said, liking the man immediately. "I understand it was you who contained the fire to the blacksmith shop last eve?"

She was rewarded by his smile. Lady Sara and Haddie had told her much about Kenshire and its people last eve, including of the man who'd once been Lord Waryn's squire and was now marshal here.

"I am sorry the shop was lost," he said. Then to Hugh, "I saw you coming, and your mounts are already prepared."

"Thank you, Reginald," Hugh said. Though it was not the marshal's duty, it seemed this man, like so many others at Kenshire, did what was necessary to run the earldom smoothly. Entire kingdoms, the French court included, could use lessons on how 'twas done so efficiently. As they bid Reginald adieu and mounted, Criseyde insisting she no longer needed assistance due to her ankle, she complimented the household, to which Hugh seemed pleased.

CECELIA MECCA

"My father is both fair and relentless, my mother giving and kind but stern when needed. The combination has made Kenshire even stronger than it was when my grandfather was alive, and even then it was a beacon of strength here in the North."

"Your parents have done well," she said, pulling her cloak tighter. "Do they accept me as easily as it seems?"

"They do, as I knew they would."

"Even your father?"

"Including my father."

"Why do you smile so? As if you are holding something back?"

"Perhaps I am," he said as they rode down a cobbled path toward the gatehouse.

"Tell me," she insisted.

"You will see soon enough," he teased.

As they passed each structure, Hugh told her of Kenshire's history and its people. They received him as warmly as she would expect for an earl's son who obviously valued each and every one of them. Criseyde attempted to ignore the looks he received from some of the ladies, no doubt more than one of whom had shared his bed.

Finally, after they reached and passed through the outer gatehouse, she could not resist. "The women look at you oddly."

"By now, all will know of you. They are likely surprised that I am to be married of my own free will."

"Hugh," she began, and then thought of how to precisely phrase her question. "At court, many husbands. . . that is to say, it is common for men to have mistresses."

Instead of answering, he simply looked at her. "Come," he called, spurring his mount forward. She was forced to

186

follow at his pace, but liked it not that he'd not answered. Did that mean Hugh wished to take a mistress? She knew it was common among the nobility, but many married for advantage. Theirs was not such a match. Criseyde's hands tightened on the reins. She would not allow it. 'Twas that simple.

But if he wanted to do so, could she stop him? Would she wish to marry a man that would do such a thing while claiming to love her? He was handsome, and an earl's son, and she'd seen the way the women looked at him...

"Hurry," he called back, approaching a small stone structure on the edge of the woods. Smoke coming from its chimney told Criseyde someone was there already.

She said nothing when Hugh helped her dismount. But the moment they entered what appeared to be a hunting cabin, Hugh locked the door. There did not appear to be anyone inside despite a fire in the hearth. With just one large bed and table with six chairs, perhaps another chamber through a closed door, it was sparse but well furnished. Looking around and removing her cloak, she was about to ask what they were doing here when Hugh removed his own cloak and sword. Then, reaching for her, his mouth met hers in a kiss like none other.

His tongue found hers, Hugh's head tilting for better access. The smell of him, the feel of his arms... Criseyde held onto his tunic tightly, wishing to get closer. In response, he broke apart from her and removed his boots. With no words, she did the same.

Shivering at the look he gave her, Criseyde no longer having any doubt why he'd brought them here, she was about to untie the strings of her kirtle when Hugh did it for her. "Take a mistress?" he asked, a harsh tone to his voice.

"I would no sooner touch another woman than reveal Wallace to King Edward."

He made quick work of her kirtle and his own tunic until Criseyde wore only a chemise, Hugh only trewes. "Nor will you touch a man other than me. Do you understand, Criseyde?"

She should have bristled at his tone, but Criseyde did not. Realizing for the first time she'd actually made him angry with the question, she allowed it, knowing Hugh was hurt.

Criseyde nodded.

The matter settled, he undressed fully and then pulled Criseyde's chemise from her body. With a groan, he kissed her again, moving them to the bed. It was warm, being close to the fire, the coverlet surprisingly soft. Without bothering to turn down the covers, Hugh moved over her, kissing everywhere.

First, her lips. And then the curve of her neck, before moving down to her breasts. Taking each nipple into his mouth as his hands explored elsewhere, Hugh showed her how outrageous her question had been.

A surge of possessiveness Criseyde hadn't known existed in her made her even more willing and ready to have Hugh inside her. She reached down, wrapped her hand around him and positioned him between her legs.

Lifting his head, he looked into her eyes, closing his own for a moment, and then wrapped his own hand around hers. He showed her how to stroke him, the sounds he made the only encouragement Criseyde needed.

"Make love to me," she said. "Now."

She got the sense he would have chuckled at her not-so-subtle request. But instead, he obeyed. Feeling her first with his finger, seemingly satisfied, he slowly entered her then.

"Dear God, Criseyde."

It was the last thing he said, Hugh not holding himself back this time. As he thrust, his hands everywhere, Criseyde met each movement with one of her own. Their rhythm together, perfection. When he leaned atop her and kissed her again, this time matching the pace of his tongue and cock that filled her so completely, and perfectly, she felt already the beginnings of a release.

"Hugh." She pulled away, knowing what was to come. "Do not pull away from me."

His nostrils flared, the command a final commitment that, without signed papers or an official betrothal, bound them together. Knowing as much, she tightened. And then let herself go. It was as if she floated above the bed for the briefest of moments until Hugh buried himself so deeply in her, Criseyde had not even realized such a thing was possible.

And then, he buried his seed in her, roaring with plea-sure and looking at her in a way that answered her question once and for all.

There would be no mistresses or lovers for either of them. Just her and her English knight, joined so perfectly and completely, as if nothing existed in the world but the two of them.

"I love you, Criseyde," he said, as if she did not know it already.

"And I love you," she said, finally able to breathe again. "Though more importantly," she said as he withdrew from her and lay on the bed beside her. "I won the bet."

It took Hugh a moment to remember, to realize what she meant. When he did, his laugh rang out in the small chamber. "Indeed, you did. But only because I came to you, saving you from asking the question. From begging me for what I knew you wanted."

She tried to swat his arm, but Hugh caught her wrist instead, smiling. "Do you remember, Criseyde, when I questioned you outside your chamber, the priest claiming he knew nothing of why you were at Bramton?"

His thumbs circled her wrist suggestively. Admittedly, she enjoyed the thought of making love again, if such a thing were possible. "I remember," she said, glad he continued his ministrations.

"You said, 'Ask me any question you like.'"

"And you responded, 'Why are you here?'"

"Indeed, to which you refused to answer. Though I hope you will be more amenable to this one."

Criseyde could not think of what question he could ask her she would not answer. His usual grin was gone, and Hugh appeared serious, as if his question were of great importance. While he waited for her answer, his hand traveled from her wrist up the length of her arm and then continued its exploration. Her pace quickened at his touch.

"What is your question?" she asked, wondering if they could discuss the matter later. For now, she could see him rise once again, Hugh not needing time to recover, it seemed.

Her future husband looked her in the eyes, neither smiling nor flinching. It must be important indeed.

"Shall I remain on top?" Hugh grinned. "Or would you like the pleasure of staring down at me? And this?" He gestured at his body. Criseyde promptly laughed, knowing this was the reason she'd fallen in love with him.

"Of course, I wish to be in charge."

He flipped them, folded his hands behind his head, and

said, "No less than I expected. I await your command, my lady."

"Just love me," she said, to which Hugh responded by pulling her down onto his chest and whispering into her ear, "Always."

EPILOGUE
BOYD

If there was anyone he'd not been expecting at Ettrick, it was the couple riding toward him. Boyd had learned this morn of an English contingency of more than twenty men scouting the perimeter of the closest village to them. Though it was nearly a full day's ride, it was too close for him, especially if the rumors were true.

Edward had planned an all-out assault on Hendralds Hill come spring. One to "put all thought of Wallace's resurrection to rest," which, for Edward, was not the first threat of its kind. Neither Boyd nor Wallace worried about such words much, but the movement of men was another matter indeed.

He'd been on lookout since before dawn and was grateful to see both his cousin and a distinctive lack of English soldiers. Emerging from the trees as he'd done once before more than a month earlier, he greeted the couple.

"Could not stay away?" he addressed Criseyde. "I've that effect on the lassies."

"How did you guess?" she asked. Unlike the last time

they'd met, there was an ease about her, about the couple, that had not been there before. Most likely it had much to do with the fact that they were now married.

"Apologies," he said to Hugh, "for not attending the wedding. There's been much talk about the earl's son marrying a ward of the French king."

Criseyde made a most unladylike sound, one his sister Laire might make. It struck him, then, the similarities between the women. Some might even consider Criseyde a spy, like his sister.

"We came for our wedding gift," Hugh teased.

"Well then," he said as they rode together, "I am sorry to disappoint you, as the only gift to be found here is me."

"You are no gift," Hugh said. "Unless you consider a bull trapped inside a hunting cabin a treasure."

It was true. Boyd was very much trapped, as was his country. Wallace, an outlaw from a king determined to route him and his supporters out, was the best hope they had now.

"Do not insult your cousin so," Criseyde chastised her husband. If you could say that was a chastisement. Though her words were of support for Boyd, her smile was for Hugh. She looked at him the same way Boyd's father Reid looked at his mother.

"I was wrong," he said to Hugh. "And will admit it." He apologized to Criseyde then. "When last you visited, I warned your husband from a wife."

Criseyde's eyes widened, but she did not seem very surprised. "Why would you do such a thing?"

"I would assure you, it had naught to do with your person," he said sincerely.

Criseyde simply smiled as they passed two men from

camp. "There are two already on the perimeter," he told them as they approached.

"Wallace wishes for two more. He will tell you in camp. There is news."

From the looks of it, the news was not good. Nor had it been for months, with the exception of Criseyde's, which had saved them from disaster.

"I met your contingency personally," he said more seriously. "The coin and men Philip promised, delivered."

"We came to ensure it was so," she said, confirming the reason they were here.

"I'd planned to come to Kenshire, for the wedding, to tell you personally, but much has happened that necessitated my presence."

"Which is precisely why we are here. Criseyde wished to hear firsthand all that has transpired. Conall was at the wedding. He spoke to Galien, who told him some."

Boyd addressed the woman responsible for all that had recently transpired. "Courtesy of your bravery in coming here to deliver the message," he said as they rode. Criseyde cut him off.

"If not me, Philip would have sent another."

"Who perhaps would not have so easily found Wallace. The English king himself has been unable to do so."

"For that," she said as they rode into the camp, "I would thank my husband."

"Would you?" Hugh asked suggestively. "I've no doubt Wallace can find a suitable chamber for the woman who provided French knights to his cause. There I can be properly thanked in many ways. Should I suggest some to you?"

"Hugh!" she chastised.

Boyd chuckled. "I'd give you his own chamber," he said, "of which you are familiar already. He is preparing a new perimeter for the men who will come when the weather breaks."

"I'd hoped to speak to him," Criseyde said.

"And you will. He should return on the morrow. Tell me. . ." They'd reached the camp. "What news from the south?"

"Besides our wedding—"

"Which I heard was a grand affair," Boyd said.

"Not of our doing," Hugh answered. "After the opportunity to plan Haydn's was stolen from them, Haddie and my mother seemed to enjoy the distraction."

"I'm certain they did." Boyd jumped from his mount and watched as Hugh assisted Criseyde from hers. With her feet on the ground, his cousin pulled his wife to him, kissed her quite thoroughly, and then turned to him.

"I'll gladly tell you all the news from Kenshire and would hear of your mission in Gurstelle Cove. First, that chamber you mentioned. To freshen ourselves, of course," he added when Boyd looked at him as if he'd gone mad. "To freshen my arse."

Though he teased his cousin, Boyd was glad for him as well. Better his cousin fall into the trap than him. Love might be for him and his brother and even Galien. But it would never, ever be for him.

Marriage, perhaps. But not love. He'd tried that once and had no need to do so again.

NEVER, ever? We'll see about that Boyd. Preorder *A Lass of His Own* on Amazon for a special release price.

Go behind the scenes with some of the history in Son of an Earl and get bonuses for all Brotherhood books by becoming a CM Insider via email or sign up here with Facebook Messages for exclusives and to chat directly with Cecelia.

GET BOOK BONUSES

Not ready for the story to end?

Go beyond the HEA with a bonus scene by subscribing to become a CM Insider.

SUBSCRIBE HERE

About the Author

Cecelia Mecca, who adores all things medieval and has loved romance since *Sweet Valley High,* can be found in Northeast Pennsylvania where she lives with her husband and two teens.

For book updates and bonuses, subscribe to be a CM Insider at CeceliaMecca.com/Insider or by using this QR code:

Also by Cecelia Mecca

Brotherhood of the Border

Kissed by the Knight

A Noble Betrayal

A Clan of Her Own

Son of a Rogue

To Love a Warrior

Border Series

Order of the Broken Blade

<u>The Blacksmith</u>

<u>The Mercenary</u>

<u>The Scot</u>

The Earl

The Chief

Kingdoms of Meria

The King's Commander

My Highland Bride

Taken by the Elderman

Her Voyager King

Time Travel

Sexy Scot

Scandalous Scot

<u>Falling for the Knight</u>

CONTEMPORARY ROMANCE

Boys of Bridgewater

Overruled by Love

Last Call

Billion Dollar Date

My Foolish Heart

PARANORMAL ROMANCE

Bloodwite

CPSIA information can be obtained
at www.ICGtesting.com
Printed in the USA
LVHW040609060922
727610LV00006B/383

9 781946 510860